Father Snoop
And
Holy Smoke

Mary Lu Warstler

Cover Picture by Charles Bell

DEDICATION

To: My family and friends
who encouraged me in so many ways.

Preface

Thank you to the many people who helped with the editing and writing of this book with their encouragement. While I cannot begin to name all those who have encouraged me, my family comes first – especially my husband and children. Many friends have also given time to edit and read. I want to especially thank my son Tim for his edits and suggestions and Pam Ritchey for the time she spent in not only editing my work but also for the time she spent in helping me to understand the process of formatting for publication. Thank you to my friend, Charles "Chuck" Bell for the cover picture.

While I am a United Methodist Pastor, I have some understanding of other denominations through my contact with different churches. Father Snoop is simply a whimsical character of my imagination as are the other characters in the book. Smoke bears some resemblance to my beloved Michael who died at about the age 19 a year ago. This is a mystery, but I hope you enjoy the fun side of it as well as the intrigue.

Book I

Snoop Meets Smoke

Prologue

Bernard William Snoop, an only child, was born to be different. From the time he was a toddler, – or maybe even before – he loved people, snooping and the outdoors. To his mother, and anyone else who found themselves the object of his curiosity, he was more often than not, referred to as Bernie Will Snoop.

Because of his great curiosity, he seemed to progress more rapidly than other children of his age, so that by the time he started school, his questions were often seen as a ploy to question authority. Needless to say, his teachers felt threatened by his insatiable quest for more things to add to his well of knowledge, especially things about which they knew very little, or nothing at all.

Other students teased him unmercifully because he was *different* He was tall for his age, not a very handsome child and unafraid of trying something new. He was a handy scapegoat for unexplained accidents, disappearing objects (like lunch sacks) and fights on the playground.

But Snoop – or Bernie – as he was generally

called – survived childhood with a minimum of scars and no less curiosity than the day he was born. Everyone – including his parents – assumed he would become a research scientist or even a private investigator. Many mouths dropped to the chin when he announced that God had called him to ministry in the church – his beloved Episcopal Church.

If, however, they thought his curiosity and snooping would stop, they were mightily mistaken. "The church and our faith are full of unanswered questions," he said. "I need to help people find ways to answer some of them."

Bernie never had much success in dating and soon lost interest in girls. Life was too full to waste time fretting about what would never be. And so, following seminary and ordination he became known among his peers as Father Bernard Snoop, a single, homely – Jimmy Durante nose, six feet three inches thin frame – vegetarian who loved small rural churches. Because he had a winning smile and a comfortable manner that drew people to him, his friends all knew he would be a good pastor.

Except for the occasional delving into *helping* local authorities solve a few mysteries – murder and mayhem – he restricted his snooping to things in nature and the workings of God and His church.

After he completed six years at his first appointment, the bishop asked Bernie to move to Oak Grove, Indiana, a small college community. With a sense of excitement and expectation, he packed up his beloved Volkswagen, said goodbye to his former parishioners – now friends – and moved.

One

Bernie arrived on an August Saturday afternoon to his new appointment, St. Peter's Episcopal Church in Oak Grove, Indiana. He loved rural settings and small towns. Having a college in that town was a bonus.

As he stood with hands in pockets, breathing in the warm summer air and taking in the sights of his new home, Bernie could feel watchful eyes upon him. He knew without turning, that someone was in his office across the alley behind him. *Probably the Women's Society ladies. Let me see, that would be...* He delved into his memory seeking names he had received and memorized...*Lois Bernhard, President, Betty Walters and Susan Raymond, committee members. By now, they know I am single and since they believe every pastor should have a good wife to help him, – they would never believe the spouse might be male because a woman shouldn't be a pastor – they will soon set out to change my marital status.*

Bernie was right, of course. They had considered every eligible widows and single women, both in the church and the community and were prepared to give the results to Father Bernie. When he went to the church, as was the custom of most pastors, to make final changes on his message, the three women met him at the door.

"Good evening, ladies," he said bowing slightly to them. "Beautiful day for moving."

"Yes it was. Welcome to our church and our community, Father Snoop. We are from the Women's Society. We needed to check on the flowers for tomorrow. I'm…" the tall, thin woman with gray hair started.

Bernie smiled and wanting to show off a little interrupted, "Let me guess, you are Lois Bernhard, president. And these are your friends and fellow committeewomen, Betty Walters and Susan Raymond."

"Why yes," said Lois her surprise sending a glow to her cheeks. "How did you know?"

Bernie laughed. "Your Senior Warden, Martin Clark sent me a pictorial directory and list of officers. And please call me Bernie or Father Bernie."

"Snoop *is* rather…eh…an unusual name."

"To some folks it is."

"Is…eh…your *wife* joining you later?" Lois didn't look at him, but found something it the corner that needed her attention.

Bernie smiled and said what he was sure they already knew, "No, I'm not married." Before they could ask if he was a widower, he added, "And I never have been."

"Oh, you poor man," said Betty.

"How can you possibly do all the things a minister does without a wife?" Susan looked shocked.

"Well, don't you worry, Father Bernie," said Lois. "We'll take care of that very soon."

"But I don't want or need a wife," he said.

"Nonsense, Father Bernie," said Lois.

"Every pastor needs a wife," said Betty.

"Who will cook and clean for you?" asked Susan.

"And who will wash and iron?" said Lois.

"I have survived since college alone," he said. "I think I can manage."

"But who will lead the women's meetings?"

"I'm sure you have many capable women who can do that very efficiently. Now if you will excuse me, I need to finish preparing for tomorrow." Bernie left them still discussing his future and retired to his study.

*   *   *

Sunday morning the women still discussed further Bernie's need for a wife. Bernie avoided them, but as he looked toward the door, the most beautiful girl he had ever seen entered, nodded to the women then went to the Sunday School class for college students. Since many of the college students came to St. Peter's, they had started a special class for them on Sunday mornings.

That beautiful girl went into the college class so she can't be more than twenty, maybe twenty-one years old. Bernie sighed. *She's much too young for me, even if she wasn't a member of my congregation.*

In spite of the facts, he felt drawn to her silky red curls, smooth complexion with a few freckles across her nose and piercing eyes like emeralds. *As her pastor, I'll have to watch myself. She almost makes me ready to change my mind about wanting a wife.*

After church, the beautiful girl joined the queue waiting to greet the new pastor. He'd seen her move to the back of the line. Finally, when the church was almost empty, she approached him and extended her hand.

"Welcome to Oak Grove, Father Snoop," she said – her voice must have come directly from the angels. Bernie felt his heart drop to his toes and blood rush to his ears. He'd seen radiant smiles before, but her face glowed with the smile that spread across her face. Her green eyes sparkled.

"I'm Miriam Parker, a student at Oak Grove College and secretary for Dr. Calvin Myers, President of the school. He knew I would be coming to church here this morning and asked me to deliver this to you." She handed him a square, white envelope.

Bernie took the envelope, trying to avoid touching her, but she almost dropped it. They both grabbed for it, entangling their fingers. The diamond on her left hand was quite noticeable. Embarrassed, he apologized. Miriam laughed and left.

Later at the manse, Bernie opened the envelope, knowing it would be a welcome invitation of some kind. Dr. and Mrs. Myers were inviting him and his wife to lunch on the following Saturday. He frowned. *Tomorrow I will have the church secretary send a reply that I will come alone. I'll have her explain that I'm a vegetarian and that I have never married.*

* * *

Bernie liked Dr. Myers and his wife, Hannah, knowing instinctively that they would become good friends. When Dr. Myers invited him to stop by his office anytime, he didn't need a second invitation.

Monday, following the Saturday luncheon, Bernie dropped by to see his new friend and have a tour of the college. But, more importantly, he wanted to see his beautiful secretary.

"Good morning, Father," said Miriam, giving him her most radiant smile.

"Good morning, Miss Parker. Is Dr. Myers

busy?" She was left-handed, so he couldn't help but notice the bare ring finger. "Your beautiful ring. Did something happen to it?"

She laughed. "No, I just realized it wasn't right for me. I returned it to its owner."

*   *   *

Bernie stopped often after that to visit with the president and his beautiful secretary. Despite the difference in their ages – ten years – Miriam pursued him. When she graduated from the college two years later, she informed Bernie she intended to marry him.

"I'm much too old for you," he said. "I will die and leave you a young widow."

She cocked her head and said, "Oh, are you God to know who will die first?"

"But, I'm as homely as a stray mutt and on a pastor's salary I could never give you the things in life you deserve."

"The only things in life I deserve are what God ordains," she said. "I love you. I want to be your wife and helpmate for as much time as God gives us to be together."

No matter the arguments, she had an answer for him. He did love her with all his heart and knew she would be perfect for him as he would be for her. The following January, she became Mrs. Bernard W. Snoop.

For ten years, she served as his wife and

helpmate in the college town they both loved. People affectionately called him *Snoop,* when he stuck his nose into legal mysteries and crimes. More often than not, his insights led to solutions. Of course, there were those who used the name in a more derogatory way, which nettled his friends. Bernie ignored them.

Early in December, Bernie received a call – a summons, actually – from this friend, Bishop John Murray. Knowing he probably wanted him to take on a new responsibility; Bernie was reluctant meet with the bishop.

Two

"Bernie, are you up?"

"Ummm," mumbled Bernie wondering if that was Miriam or an angel of mercy calling to him. Opening one eye, he saw only the ceiling – both eyes open gave little more view. A cold breeze from the one-inch space between his window and the windowsill sent him back under the covers.

"Bernie?"

"I'm up." The muffled words from beneath the blanket belied his statement.

Hmmm, what is that I smell? Bernie pulled his head from beneath the thick, blue comforter and sniffed. *Coffee. Miriam must be ready for breakfast.* He sniffed again as if the bold Columbian aroma would send caffeine into his veins through his nose. *After all, this Jimmy Durante schnozzle ought to be good for something.*

Lying still, he waited. Nothing. No jolt of caffeine. Not even a taste on the back of his tongue. "Ah, well," he mumbled to himself, "guess not."

Casting the comforter aside, he sat on the side of the bed and scooted his feet around the green shag rug beside the bed in search of his slippers.

As if she knew what he was doing, Miriam called from the foot of the stairs. "Your slippers are in the closet and your robe is on the closet door hook. Don't forget to close the window."

How does she always know? Bernie grinned. *Because she's my beautiful wife.*

Without further delay, Bernie opened the closet, slipped his feet into the lamb's wool lined moccasins and pulled on his maroon flannel robe he'd worn for ten years. Miriam had given it to him their first Christmas together.

Tying the threadbare sash, he followed the coffee aroma down the stairs as if it were a finger beckoning him on. He heard a thump on the porch as he hit the bottom step. He detoured, shuffled to the front door, opened it and retrieved the morning newspaper before the blowing snow covered it.

Carefully he unfolded the damp Oak Grove Gazette read the headline and groaned. Miriam came into the room as he threw the newspaper down on the couch. She gave him a questioning look and picked it up.

"A little damp this morning?" she asked turning to the front page. "Oh," she said then read the big, bold print, "Father Snoop Does It Again." She glanced at Bernie and continued to read, "Father Bernard Snoop from St. Peter's Episcopal Church has once again snooped into police business and helped them bag a syndicated drug operation which allegedly includes Councilman Jake Lester. It seems that the council member's speeches against our teens and the arrest of several Junior and Senior high school students were all a smoke screen to hide his own part in providing the drugs. Father Snoop's nose ended that little game and cleared the accused teens of any wrongdoing. Councilman Lester is in Oak Grove County Jail awaiting his hearing. No bond had been set as of press time this morning. Father Snoop once again worked with the police in bringing peace to our community."

Miriam cleared her throat and placed her hand over her twitching lips. Bernie hated any kind of attention – and especially attention related to his bent for *snooping*. But, she knew he could never stop snooping when the lives of innocent people were at stake. Two of the arrested teens were from his congregation.

"Go ahead, laugh," he said. "Silly jerks at the newspaper. They don't even give credit to the police department who did all the work and put their lives on the line."

"Maybe you need to take out a full page ad and declare you innocence," said Miriam letting a small laugh escape, unable to keep the twinkle from her eyes.

"Miriam…" Bernie wanted to sound stern, but

when his beautiful wife looked at him like that, he melted. "I guess they do give our police credit, but I wish they would leave me out of it."

"Then stop snooping."

"Yeah sure, I will when I stop breathing. I've got a *snooping gene* in my makeup – and not just in the genetic heredity."

Miriam laughed, laid the paper aside and slipped into his embrace. She kissed him soundly and clung to him for a minute.

"How could I be so lucky to find such a beautiful, caring wife?"

"It wasn't luck, Bernard Snoop. I worked hard to catch you."

"Yes, you did, didn't you?" He kissed her again. "You don't know how many times I have thanked God for your persistence."

"And me for your willingness to be caught. Now, we better have breakfast before it gets cold."

"How cold can cold cereal get?" Bernie grinned.

"I have eggs for you this morning. Since we have to make a trip to Metropolis and the weather station is calling for more snow, I thought we might need a little extra protein to keep us going."

"Then let's get to them before they become dried up and we have to crumble them on our toast."

They laughed and started for the kitchen, the

paper forgotten.

*   *   *

Breakfast over, Bernie showered and dressed then went to his study to work while Miriam dressed for their trip to Metropolis – a trip he would rather not take. He stood looking around the room as if it were the first time he'd ever seen it – or would be the last. The traditional oak roll-top desk with all its slots and drawers that had served so many pastors – no one knew for sure how many – stood guard over the wall of books to the left and the window to the right. On the other side of the window was Bernie's, very much used, one time plush, recliner. It had been his father's and even though the parsonages he had lived in so far were furnished, he insisted he had to have his *thinking* chair. Some day he would get it redone, but for now, it fit the room.

Easing into its softness, avoiding the loose spring on the left side of the seat, Bernie closed his eyes, letting his troubled thoughts swirl, as if drawing him into a churning eddy.

He was going to Metropolis today because his good friend, John – now Bishop John Murray – had asked him to come. Since he'd said nothing about his wife Joanna joining them and since he asked them to meet at his office, Bernie could only assume the worst. John was going to ask him to move.

It had been twelve years since he came to St. Peter's – for the most part, twelve *good* years. On occasion, he allowed himself to become involved in mysterious investigations, but then he would do that no matter where he was. It was his nature to be curious and to want justice.

*   *   *

Miriam knocked on the study door then opened it. "Are you ready to go?"

"It's only eight-thirty. Our appointment is for eleven."

"Bernie, it's a two hour drive in good weather. Have you looked out the window lately?"

"Yes, I did. I was thinking about taking a quick walk around the block. I love to walk in a snowstorm. Want to go with me?" Bernie stood, took her hand and raised it to his lips.

"Bernie," Miriam said, "you're procrastinating."

"I know." He grinned. "Oh well, I guess the walk will have to wait. Are we taking the bug?" Bernie laughed at the face Miriam made. She didn't like his '69 Volkswagen to begin with and in a snowstorm yet!

"All right," he said. "Let me get my coat. We'll take your Chevy."

"Here's your coat." Miriam held it for him as he slipped his arms into the sleeves.

Three

Bernie sat in the car for a few seconds quietly staring at the garage wall. Miriam laid her hand on his arm. Finally, he sighed, opened the garage door, started the car and backed out onto the already white driveway.

"It will be all right, Bernie," she said.

"I know," said Bernie, "but…" He backed onto the street and sighed again.

Quarter-sized white flakes had already covered the windshield, melting to streams of water. He switched on the wipers and slowly moved the car down the street watching for neighborhood children playing in the white stuff.

Thanksgiving was over and sounds of Christmas filled the air. Lawns already sported Santa and his reindeer, Frosty the Snowman and here and there a large crèche. Fake icicles hung from eaves and strings of multicolored lights wrapped around bushes and trees like loosely knitted shawls. Falling snow heightened the Christmas mood – at least according to the traffic. It seemed to Bernie that everyone was out

Christmas shopping – at least he assumed that was the reason for so much traffic. He wanted to feel the Christmas spirit, but until he talked with John, he would be apprehensive.

Pulling onto the expressway, Bernie headed northeast to Metropolis. Miriam turned on the radio to hear Christmas music. Instead, she got some excitable young weather reporter. "While we have no official weather advisory yet, the snow is falling. Surely, we'll have a white Christmas this year. So far the roads are clear, but folks, be careful while you're out there shopping."

"White Christmas? It is barely December," grumbled Bernie. "They ought to be telling folks to stay off the roads, not to run out and do their shopping."

"Bernie, don't be such a Scrooge," said Miriam. She smiled at his sour look then said,

"We can always go back and call John. Tell him we can't make it because of the weather."

"We'll make it," he said sure that Miriam knew he would never turn back. "I just don't understand what's so important that we need to go to Metropolis at the beginning of one of our busiest times of the year to say nothing of this blizzard. Why does John want us to drive to *his* office?" Bernie said. "We could have met him half-way."

"Bernie, you've been stewing over this ever

since he called. He couldn't possibly have known it would snow today. That's not what's bothering you, is it?"

"Miriam…"

"You're afraid he's going to ask you to move and he might do that. But, it's in God's hands, Bernie. Whatever comes we're together."

"But, Miriam, Oak Grove is your home. You've never lived anywhere else."

"Bernie, my home is where *you* are."

They were approaching the off ramp to Metropolis, so Bernie turned his attention to exiting the freeway and getting on the right street.

"Whatever he has to say, he could have come to us or talked on the phone. He knows I don't like city driving."

Miriam smiled at her agitated husband. "Bernie, I know you would have preferred your VW, but…"

"It's not that, Miriam. Sure, I prefer my little bug, but your Chevy was a better choice for this trip. I just don't…"

"John is a busy man, Bernie. After all he *is* the Bishop of a large area."

"And I'm not a busy man?"

"Of course you are, but he…he is…"

"I know. More important. He's my boss. He calls the shots. But, I thought he was also my friend."

"He *is* your friend, but he has a lot on his mind

with the death of Father Jones at St. Mark's in Metropolis. That has to be difficult for the people of the church as well as John. They'll have to go through the Christmas season without pastoral leadership."

"I know you're right Miriam and I'm sorry I'm such a grouch. But you know how I hate driving in the city traffic. I could never live here. And my *snoopy sense* is warning me that something is going to happen that I won't like."

Miriam laughed.

She knows I like to grumble. No need to remind her that when my snoopy sense kicks in, I can usually expect trouble.

Bernie, watching the traffic in the four-lane streets, tried to keep his mind off the move he was sure John was prepared to offer. Bishop or friend, John would not have called him to Metropolis this time of year without a serious reason.

"What happened to Father Jones?" Miriam asked thankfully breaking into his musings.

"The official report said he fell down a flight of steps in the church and broke his neck."

"And the unofficial report?" Miriam cocked her head and glanced over at him. "I know you've been doing some research."

Bernie laughed. "You don't miss much do you? You're right. Something seems all wrong with the picture. How could a man fall down a flight of steps that he's used for over twenty years?"

"Bernie, people fall in their homes all the time."

"Yes, but rumor has it there might be foul play."

"Whose rumor?"

"I have my sources."

"I suppose John wants you to look into it."

Bernie jerked around so quickly, he almost missed his turn onto the parking garage street. "Why would you say that?"

"Because John knows you as well as I do. You can't stand an unsolved mystery – even if it's none of your business."

"But if there was foul play, it is my business. Susan and Bill Jones were friends and colleagues of mine. Susan has the right to know what happened to her husband. And the church has a right to know if someone is taking pot-shots at their pastors."

"Bernie...never mind. John is the bishop. He will handle it."

Bernie signaled and turned right then left into the parking deck of the city building next door to the bishop's office. The city had agreed to provide three free parking spots in their garage since the church was renting the entire 22nd floor of the building. Bernie pulled into spot number three. John's black Lincoln and his secretary's blue Toyota already occupied spaces one and two.

Taking Miriam's hand, Bernie followed the

long covered bridge from the parking deck across the busy street to the lobby. No matter how many times he came to this building – which wasn't often – the spaciousness of it awed him, along with the polished marble floors, the exquisite sparkling fountain in the center of the room and all the paintings by famous artists arranged on the walls with spotlights to highlight them.

"Don't they worry about theft?" he mused aloud then pushed the up button. The elevator doors slid open with hardly a sound. Feeling Miriam's fingers squeeze his, he answered his own question. "Oh well, not my problem."

Four

The elevator opened into the lobby of the Bishop's office. Although Bernie had been to John's office on several occasions, the expanse of the room never failed to impress him. Gold carpet with flecks of brown, black and orange spread from wall to wall. Stepping out of the elevator, he had to look down at his feet. Although he knew better, he felt as if he had stepped on a cluster of marshmallows.

Directly opposite the elevator, the whole wall was glass overlooking the busy streets of Metropolis. Gold draperies framed the outer edges allowing more light into the room. Snow swirling by the window outside reminded him of how high they were and how far the snow had to go to join the other flakes already gathered on the ground.

Left of the elevator was wall-to-wall, ceiling to floor, shelves filled with books and assorted bric-a-brac. On either side of the elevator, pictures on loan from the museum took up the wall space. This month they were featuring Currier and Ives Christmas scenes. Next month would be something different.

To the left, was the door to John's office, guarded by his secretary Clarice Maloney, who had been a part of the office since the first bishop – well maybe only the last thirty or forty years. She had to be pushing sixty, but to be honest she didn't look a day older than forty-nine.

Clarice glanced up and replaced the frown at her computer by a smile for her visitors. She looked as if she were glad to be away from that monstrous machine on her desk.

"Good morning Father Snoop, Miriam. Bishop John was afraid you wouldn't make it with the weather like it is."

"Did we have a choice?" Bernie's sarcasm fell on deaf ears and Clarice continued in her prattle as if he hadn't spoken. "Is it as bad as it looks out there?"

"Worse," said Bernie.

Miriam laughed and said, "It's bad, but if you're careful you can get around."

"Well, I hope it clears before I leave."

"When is that? I didn't think you worked on Saturdays." Bernie felt his snoopy antennae swirling in all directions. *This must be really bad if he asked Clarice to come in on her day off – in a snowstorm yet!*

"I'm only here until noon today. We had some catching up to do. Why don't you two have a seat and I'll see if he's ready for you."

"I'm sure he's ready for us. He said eleven o'clock and it's that time now."

"Bernie..."

"I know, Miriam." He smiled down at her. "He's a busy man."

Clarice came back to them. "Bishop will see you now. Would you like some coffee or tea?"

"Some coffee would be nice," said Miriam. "Black."

"Father?"

"No thanks."

"If you will go right in, I'll bring your coffee in just a minute."

Bernie paused in the doorway, taking in another expansive room – about half the size of the lobby. A dark cherry desk big enough for six people to work at the same time; two black leather, wing-backed chairs facing the desk filled one end of the room. A matching leather couch at the opposite end of the room with a cherry writing table that served double duty as a coffee table in front of it balanced the room. The table was slightly smaller than the almost six and a half feet long desk. Still there was a sense of spaciousness. A fireplace glowed on the outer wall, giving an appearance of warmth and hospitality. Bernie felt neither. The fireplace was fake and his friend looked more *Bishop* than *friend* today.

Miriam nudged him. He blinked and moved toward the bishop who rose to meet them – his hand extended in greeting.

"Bernie, Miriam, it's so good to see you," said John. He shook Bernie's hand and gave Miriam a peck on the cheek.

"John," said Bernie acknowledging the bishop. "It's been a while."

"How are you doing, Miriam? I can't believe you are still with this joker. How long's it been? Six years?"

"Almost ten, John," answered Miriam. She smiled at his embarrassment of not remembering.

"Has it been that long? My how time…"

"Yes, time does get away from us," said Miriam. "How is Joanna? We were hoping to have time for lunch after our meeting."

"She's well, Miriam, but she has a luncheon engagement with the Professional Women's Organization. She was disappointed when I told her you were coming."

"Well, tell her we missed her. Maybe next time."

"John, you didn't call us here just to chit-chat. There's a blizzard blowing and we…"

"Bernie," Miriam took one of the black wing backed chairs.

"You've got something on your mind," said

Bernie, "so out with it."

"You always were one to go right to the heart of the matter and...sit down and..."

Bernie glared, but sat in the other wing backed chair."

"Yes, well...you're right. I've been watching you and your work. You are really an excellent pastor. You are kind and caring and..."

"John, we went to school together. Don't try to give me a snow job. There's enough of that out there." Bernie nodded toward the window behind the bishop's desk. "What do you want?"

"I want you to go to St. Mark's here in Metropolis."

"John you know I hate city living. Whatever possessed you to even think of me for that position?"

"Bernie, their pastor had been there for over twenty years."

"I understand that. I heard he died as the result of an accident?"

"He fell down the steps in the church and broke his neck. The people are taking it hard. He was their friend. They loved him."

"Do you believe that? That he fell down the stairs, I mean? Stairs that he'd gone up and down for over twenty years."

"Bernie people fall all the time."

"I suppose, but did he? Anyway, what does that

have to do with me?"

Ignoring the initial question, John answered the second. "They need someone to help them through their grief. You're really good at that."

"But, John, you know how much I hate…"

"Miriam, talk to him."

"Sorry, John. I'll go wherever Bernie goes, but I'll never try to influence him."

"Bernie, it will only be an interim position until they work through their grief. Then if you want to stay, we'll work on it. If you want to move, we'll find a place more to your liking."

"How long is *interim?*"

"As long as it takes to get the work done." John gave Bernie a look that clearly said that the work was more than just helping a grieving congregation.

"What about the folks at St. Peter's?"

"We'll send Harold Peterson there. You know Harold. He's got a lot of charisma. He'll work out fine."

"Why not send him to St. Mark's?"

"Because he doesn't have the patience you have with people who are grieving."

"You mean they're angry and they need someone with a thick skin."

"I wouldn't say that."

"Of course you wouldn't. Let us think about it, pray about it and talk it over. We'll get back to you.

How soon do you have to know? How soon would we have to move?"

"They need someone during the Christmas season."

"John, it will be bad enough to leave St. Peter's after twelve years. I couldn't think of leaving on such short notice and at the Christmas season when everything is planned."

"Father Jones did."

"He had no choice. I do."

The two men stared at each other. Finally, Bishop Murray laughed. "You always could outstare me. All right, you could begin the first Sunday of the New Year."

"I'll call you in a day or two," said Bernie rising. "Miriam, let's see if we can get out of this horrendous traffic and treacherous streets before we stop somewhere for lunch."

"Why don't you stay over," said John. "We'll put you up in the Hilton and pay for your meals."

"Are you really *that* desperate? Thanks, but no thanks. Tomorrow is the first Sunday of Advent. I need to be in Oak Grove."

Bernie and Miriam left the bishop chewing on his fingernail. Bernie knew that meant he was extremely anxious. *But, why me? I hate cities. I hate the traffic. I love my church and the people in Oak Grove. But, John knows I have a knack for snooping. He would never ask, but is that the hidden agenda in this move?*

Although he would not make a commitment without talking it over with Miriam, Bernie knew before he left John's office he would be at St. Mark's the first Sunday of January – the day before his and Miriam's tenth wedding anniversary.

Five

Early January, always unpredictable, began with clouds hanging low on that first Saturday. By the time the moving truck – too small to be a moving van – arrived in Metropolis, the sun was playing peek-a-boo with the clouds. Wind had picked up, making the thirty-five degrees feel much colder.

Bernie and Miriam had followed the truck in separate cars – she in her blue Chevy and he in his beloved '69 yellow Volkswagen. As Bernie got out of the car, he noticed two young boys on the sidewalk watching, apparently so interested in the truck that they didn't see Bernie.

"How come it's such a small truck, Tommy?" asked the smaller boy, looking up at the other boy. His red stocking cap covered his forehead almost to his eyes. He pushed it back with soggy mittened hands. His parka was unzipped leaving the coat open to the wind. Both boys had a dimpled chin and were dressed similarly. They looked enough alike to have been twins, except for the size.

"I don't know, Sam. Maybe preachers can't afford much furniture," answered Tommy. "Zip your coat. You want to take pneumonia?"

Sam pulled at the zipper until he finally got the coat closed. "Why don't we ask that man who's getting out of the truck?"

"Yeah, why don't we?" Tommy moved over to the driver of the truck. "Hey mister. What you got on that truck?"

The truck driver loomed over the boys, hands on hips and glared. "Get lost kids. We got furniture and stuff to unload."

"Whose furniture is it?" Sam asked.

"Scram."

"I bet it's another preacher," said Tommy.

"Hope he don't fall down steps like the other one did."

"Don't be goofy. Anybody can fall."

"Yeah, but preachers are supposed to be careful."

"Yeah, well, he wasn't."

"Hey kids, move it before we drop something on you."

Tommy and Sam moved aside but continued to watch the two men carry boxes and the few pieces of furniture into the house. Bernie and Miriam approached from around the truck.

"Hey," said Sam. "Maybe he's the new preacher."

"Maybe," said his brother. "I'll ask," he said

moving closer to Bernie.

"Hi," said the older boy. "I'm Tommy. You moving in here?"

"Yes, we are," said Bernie, stooping to be on a level with the boys.

"This is my brother Sam. We live in that big house on the corner. What's your name?"

"My name is Bernie and this is my wife Miriam," he said nodding to Miriam who stood beside him.

"She's pretty," said Sam.

"Why, thank you," answered Miriam.

"You the new preacher at St. Mark's?"

"Yes, I am. You go there?"

"Yeah, when Mom gets us up in time. How come you don't have much furniture?"

"The church provides a furnished manse, which means all the basics are there. We just have a few favorite pieces that belong to us. It makes moving easier."

"Yeah, won't take so long to unpack."

"That's right."

"Father Jones died." Tommy was a kid who seemed to speak his mind. Bernie liked that.

"I know. What happened to him?" Bernie sensed this child could probably give him more information than most adults would.

"He fell down some stairs at the church," said Sam.

"I think someone pushed him," said Tommy.

"Why do you think that?"

"Cause he was a basketball player. He knew how to move without falling."

"Very interesting," said Bernie. Miriam smiled, shook her head and went to supervise the movers.

"She don't believe me, does she?" Tommy looked in Bernie's eye for truth.

"Let's just say, she's a little skeptical."

"But you're not specktical, are you? You believe me. I can see it in your eyes."

"Well, young fellow, my full name is Bernard W. Snoop and my friends tell me I live up to my name."

The boys giggled. "I never heard anyone with a name like Snoop before. Are you teasing us?" Tommy narrowed his eyes and glared at Bernie.

"Nope. That's my name."

"Will you find out who pushed Father Jones?" Tommy's eyes were wide with awe and a touch of sadness. "He was our friend."

"If someone pushed him, Tommy, I'll find out. It might take me a while, but I'll find out."

"Thank you, Father Bernie. We won't tell anyone you're snooping so the killer won't come after you."

"I appreciate that boys and if you hear anything of interest, you know where I live."

"Okay…oops, there's Mom on the porch. She told us to stay home."

"Then you better scoot. Give me five before you go."

"Okay!' The boys giggled again, slapped their palms against his and ran for home. Bernie stood and watched them cross the street. They turned around and waved. He waved back.

Six

Bernie stuffed his hands in his pockets and shuffled through the slush to make sure the movers didn't damage any of his possessions – as if he had anything worth worrying about. He watched while they took their few belongings into the house. Miriam would show the men where to put things. The sun and cloud mix was quickly turning to all clouds – black, threatening ones at that. *Could mean rain or snow, given the temperature. Probably snow for my first Sunday at St. Mark's.*

The truck left and Bernie moved the cars into the garage. *At least we have an attached double garage with a door to the kitchen.* Wind and rain pounded the garage door, reminding him it was January. He stepped into the kitchen expecting to see Miriam fixing lunch. He was surprised to find, not his beautiful wife, but a short, pudgy woman with graying hair that seemed to have a life of its own. Confused he said, "Hello."

"Good afternoon, Father Bernie, or would you rather I call you Father Snoop?"

"Either is fine," said Bernie still feeling as if he

had walked into the wrong house for lunch. "Bernie seems easier for most folks."

The woman laughed, a soft gentle hee, hee, hee. "I'm sorry," she said. "You must wonder why a strange woman is in your kitchen. I'm Charlotte Lane. I've been housekeeper for this manse for over thirty years. Apparently no one told you I come with the house." Charlotte laughed again then added, "Of course, if you don't want me…"

"You're right. No one told me, so I'm a little surprised," said Bernie. "Have you talked to my wife?"

"Yes, I did poor dear. She is a beautiful woman and a hard worker, but she seemed feverish to me. She shouldn't have been out in this weather. I sent her to bed. I'm making her some tea and toast for lunch."

Bernie felt himself pale. "She was all right this morning. Miriam is never sick. Where is she? I'd better go check on her. Do you think she needs a doctor?"

"I would guess it is just that twenty-four hour flu virus that's going around, but I know you must feel anxious in a new place and all. I can call Dr. Stevens if you want. He's my doctor – one of the few who make house calls on occasion."

"Why don't you do that, Charlotte? I'd feel much better knowing it's nothing serious."

Bernie climbed the stairs and hurried to the side

of the bed. He laid his hand on Miriam's feverish brow. "Miriam? Why didn't you tell me you were sick? We could have waited to move."

"I was all right this morning. It started about the time we got here. Bernie, I'm sorry I'm not much help."

"Don't you worry about that. Charlotte is calling a doctor."

"Bernie, I don't need a doctor. I just feel tired and something upset my stomach."

"You were throwing up? Miriam!"

"I'm all right. I…"

There was a tap on the door and Charlotte stuck her head into the room. "Dr. Stevens is here, Father. Shall I send him up?"

"No," said Miriam.

"Yes," said Bernie at the same time. "Please show him up Charlotte."

She left and returned a minute or so later with Dr. Stevens. Bernie stood and didn't have to look down on the man with a graying mustache to match his hair. He was as tall as Bernie.

"Glad to meet you Father. Sorry you need my services so soon, but I'm glad I was available and don't live far from here. He shook Bernie's hand then moved toward the bed. "Now, let's see about our patient. When did you begin to feel ill?"

Bernie and Charlotte stood by the door anxious

to do something to help. After poking, prodding and checking all the vital signs, Dr. Stevens stood and addressed Miriam. "There's a lot of this going around, Mrs. Snoop. It's a twenty-four hour bug. I'll give you something for the nausea and fever, but you'll just have to ride it out. You should be fine by Monday morning, or Monday noon at the latest. Call me if you're not."

"Thank you Dr. Stevens. I appreciate you coming out in the storm." Miriam tried to smile but found she had to squint as if her eyes wouldn't focus.

"I was on my way home anyway. I just live a couple of blocks from here. You get some rest now."

"I'll be back and check on you in a little bit," said Bernie as he started to follow the doctor out of the room.

"Okay..." Miriam was already drifting off to sleep.

After the doctor left, Bernie tried to eat because Charlotte had done her best to fix him a vegetarian lunch. He was drinking his second cup of coffee when Charlotte came into the dining room.

"Since no one told you about me, maybe we need to talk," she said.

"I think that's a good idea," said Bernie. "Why don't you join me for coffee?"

Charlotte hesitated, then went to the kitchen and

returned with another cup. "Thank you," she said.

"Now, fill me in on what you do besides take care of my ailing wife." Bernie smiled at her and watched her slowly relax as she sipped her coffee.

"I started here when I was a teenager – just out of high school. I've always loved cleaning and cooking. In the past, I came in from six to six, Monday through Friday. Sometimes I work on Saturday until noon, or longer if needed. I have Sunday's off, unless needed. I do cleaning, cooking and grocery shopping. Mrs. Jones didn't like to do any of that. I'm flexible, if Mrs. Snoop wants to do her own cooking and cleaning. If you don't want me at all, I'll…I'll…find something else."

"Charlotte, I'm sure my wife – and please call her Miriam – will be glad to have you here. You'll have to talk to her when she's feeling better to know what she wants. But until she's better, I definitely need you."

"I'll stay until six today to help put things away and fix dinner. Then I'll come back in the morning to stay with Miriam while you are at the church. I'll work out time off with you later."

"Thank you Charlotte. And don't worry about me for dinner. I'm not a true vegetarian. I can eat meat. I just don't care much for it. I'll eat whatever your fix. Miriam might want some more tea and toast."

"I have a small chicken in the refrigerator that I was going to put on for dinner. Maybe I'll boil it and make chicken soup for her."

"She would love that," said Bernie smiling. Beaming, Charlotte left the room.

Long after Charlotte departed, Bernie sat staring into his cup while his coffee got cold. *What a way to begin a new appointment. I hope there's nothing too important next week. Monday is our anniversary. I'd like to do something special with Miriam if she is feeling up to it.*

Seven

Although the fever was gone, Bernie insisted that Miriam stay home Sunday morning. He fluffed the pillows that surrounded her. Tears filled her eyes as she took Bernie's hand.

"This is your first Sunday in a new church and I should be with you. What will people think?"

"Miriam, since when have you worried about what people think? You need to stay right where you are so you can get better. If you feel up to it, we'll celebrate tomorrow. If not, we will postpone the celebration until you feel better. I will be in this church more than one Sunday. You'll be with me the rest of the Sundays."

Bernie grinned at her, but deep within he felt that *Snoopy sense* kick in and wondered what that meant. Would he not stay? Would they not want him? To hide the sudden fear he felt wrapping around his very bones, Bernie leaned over to kiss her.

"Be careful," she said. "You don't want to get what I've got."

"Then we can suffer together," he said and

kissed her again.

"Bernie, just remember they need you and I'm here praying for you."

"I will. Now, you rest. Charlotte is here to take care of you and make sure I get something to eat, so don't you worry about a thing. I'm going over early to get a feel for the building, find my office and all that good stuff."

Bernie went to the garage with a feeling of uneasiness. *People are sometimes angry in their grief, but how much will they let that anger rule? Maybe I would rather not know.* He sighed and climbed into his VW. Miriam wanted him to take her Chevy, but he needed the assurance of his reliable old friend – even if that friend was made of metal and ran on wheels instead of legs.

Rain mixed with snow had lasted all night, leaving the streets and sidewalks slushy and slick. He would have preferred to walk, but didn't need to take a chance of falling – not today anyway. The church was only three blocks away, so he was there within minutes even with the bad roads.

Bernie parked across the street where he sat gazing at his new place of worship. St. Mark's was a large gray stone building on the corner of Long and 32nd Streets. A three-story office building occupied the lot next to the church on 32nd Street. A narrow alley ran between the two buildings from 32nd to 31st Streets. Charlotte had told him there was a door from his office to the alley if he didn't want to go into the main part of the church. This morning, however, he wanted to see the sanctuary first.

On the corner, facing Long Street and 32nd was the Baptist Church – a large red brick building. Each church had a parking lot next to the church on Long Street. Bernie parked in the spot marked *Pastor* and walked around to the main entrance. While the parking lot was virtually empty, he found several folks already in the sanctuary. Martha Williams, a slim woman with short, gray hair had been the organist at St. Mark's for thirty years. Joel Prichard, a young man fresh out of college was the music coordinator. He was beginning his third year at St. Mark's. Les Jenkins a man almost as tall and thin as Bernie, balding with only a half ring of hair around his ears and neck was the Junior Warden/custodian who took pride in his work.

After introductions, Les Jenkins took Bernie to his office. They walked through the narthex to a corridor that ran the entire length of the sanctuary and beyond. Sometime along the years of the church's existence, the church fathers had shortened the width of the sanctuary and added the corridor, one wall of which was the row of stained glass windows. The other wall became the divider between the sanctuary and the corridor. At the end, another hall veered to the right – behind the sanctuary. They walked past doors to the secretary's office and the Choir Room. At the end was the Pastor's Study – a corner room with one side facing the hall, one facing the alley, the third facing 32nd Street and the fourth opened into a short tunnel-like hallway that split in two. To the right was a door that led to the sanctuary pulpit area. To the left, a wooden railing surrounded the stairs that led down to the basement kitchen.

"Be careful of those stairs, Father," said Les. "That's where Father Jones fell."

Bernie repressed a shiver. "Thank you Mr. Jenkins, both for the tour and the warning."

"Quite all right, Father. You can call me Les if you want to. He stood silent for a moment.

"Is there something else, Les?" Bernie gave the man his full attention, sensing he was troubled about something.

"Father…we…the congregation all loved Father Jones and his family."

Bernie waited. This was a known fact. Les had more to say.

"I…," Les swallowed hard as if forcing his emotions to recede. "I take good care of this building. It's God's house and I revere it as such."

"I'm sure you do, Les. All that I've seen is in perfect order." *What is the man trying to say?*

"Father Jones used these back stairs every day –

sometimes several times a day. He kept a pot of coffee in the kitchen."

Ah, thought Bernie. "And you're wondering how he could suddenly slip and fall to his death?"

Les looked up at Bernie, moisture gathering in his eyes. "Yes, Sir. Did I do something that caused him to fall?"

"Like what, Les? People trip and fall all the time – even in their homes."

"I know, but I had just cleaned the stairs – washed them down. Maybe they were still wet and…"

"Did you tell him they were wet?"

"Oh yes. I even put an orange construction-type cone at the top."

"Then I'm sure he would have been very cautious."

"That's what I thought until…" Les took two deep breaths.

"Until what, Les?"

"When they found him, the cone wasn't there and I can't help wondering if I only thought I put it out. Father, did I cause his death?"

The anguish on Les' face touched Bernie's heart. "Les, you did tell him, didn't you?"

"Oh, yes. I'm sure I told him."

"Did you ever forget the cone before?"

"No. I'm always careful about things like that."

"Where was the cone when they found Father Jones?"

"In my supply closet."

"Where you always keep it?"

Les looked blank then paled. "There's a shelf for it in the closet, but it was just lying in there as if I had thrown it in and closed the door to keep it from falling out."

Bernie smiled. "If I were a betting man, I would bet my first paycheck that your closet is as clean and organized as the rest of this building."

Les grinned. "That it is, Sir. If the closet isn't organized, it would take much longer to do my job." He thought for a minute. "But, that would mean someone else moved the cone and threw it in my closet."

"Maybe they thought the stairs were dry and the cone was in the way."

"That's a possibility I never thought about."

"I think you can rest assured that you had nothing to do with his fall. People sometimes get careless with familiar routines."

"Yes Sir, though I can't see Father Jones ever being careless. But, I'm sure glad I didn't cause his accident. Thank you Father Bernie. I'll go now and leave you to your work."

"Thanks again, Les," said Bernie as he returned to his office, a nagging prickle that told him someone moved that cone on purpose. Why?

Setting aside his *snoopy sense,* Bernie settled down to review his morning message and to pray for guidance. A tap at the door startled him. Les opened it and said, "Ms. Williams will be beginning the processional in five minutes."

"Thank you, Les. I'll be right there."

Eight

All in all that first service went well. The choir sounded good, he thought the sermon was a little above average and everyone seemed to be listening. After greeting folks at the door, Bernie started back to his office to remove his vestments. He noticed a trio of folks wearing frowns and pursed lips waiting near the door. *I don't remember greeting them. They must want something.* He hardly was within earshot when one of the men raised his voice.

"Father, we *need* to talk to you." Bernie tried in vain to remember their names.

"I'm Chuck Lewis, the Senior Warden," said the man who must have been a star quarterback somewhere in his past. He was shorter than Bernie, maybe five-eight. His salt and pepper hair tended to curl across his head, giving him a somewhat boyish look. His dark, flashing eyes and square chin emphasized by the tightly clamped teeth told Bernie he was looking for trouble. *Grief I expect – even anger. But this is pure rage.*

"Why don't we go in my office?" said Bernie taking a step toward the door, but Mr. Lewis was not going to wait for any niceties.

"You didn't announce the board meeting for tomorrow night," Lewis continued.

"I'm sorry. I didn't know about a board meeting tomorrow night. I just moved in yesterday."

"That's no excuse," said Lewis. "I'm sure the bishop gave you materials about our regular meetings."

"If he did, they are still packed. I assumed that so soon after the holidays, there would be little happening the first week. Tomorrow is my wedding anniversary and I had planned to celebrate with my wife."

"Where *is* your wife?" the tall, thin woman spoke as if he had lied about having a wife. "We expect the pastor's wife to *always* be at his side when he greets us after the service. And certainly we expect her to perform her duties as the pastor's wife at our women's meetings."

"And that would be when? And what duties do you expect?" Bernie tried to keep his temper under control. These folks were out for blood – his blood. He would just have to ride out the storm for now.

"We meet the second Tuesday of each month, which is this Tuesday. We expect her to be the hostess and serve for our afternoon tea."

"I'm sorry, Ms....?"

"It's *Mrs.* Mrs. Malcolm Sinclair."

"I'm sorry Mrs. Sinclair, but Miriam in down with the flu this morning. I'm not sure she will be up to serving tea Tuesday. If you will call her Tuesday morning…"

"I will not call her. She can call me if she will not be there. Otherwise we expect to see her."

Bernie let the venomous tone of the order slide. Miriam would talk to her. She could hold her own with the women. Of that, he was certain. He turned his attention back to Chuck Lewis.

"Mr. Lewis, about the board meeting, can we postpone it for a week? Surely, so close after the holidays there can't be much to discuss, except possibly the Lenten services. The worship committee can take care of that."

"We *never* change board meetings to satisfy our personal desires. *I'm* not even going to be here. I have a conference in California that I need to attend. Don't you think *I* would rather be here for the board meeting?"

"I think that's all the more reason for changing the night. You should certainly be here."

"As long as I am Senior Warden, the meetings will *not* be changed. It will go on as scheduled. My wife, Patricia, will chair the meeting in my absence. I have to be at that conference in California."

The third member of the advance scouting party, as Bernie considered the group, had been standing by wordlessly. A well-dressed, up-scale man, not more than five-five, he carried himself like a CEO of a successful company. He stepped forward to enter the discussion – or put an end to it.

"I hope you understand Father that we need to keep things as they were in order to get through our grief. We've had too much upset. We can't handle any more."

"I understand, Mr....?"

"I'm Malcolm Sinclair. I would think you would know that by now."

Ah yes, The Sinclairs from Sinclair Savings and Loan. He forced his attention back to Sinclair's words.

"Lewis and I are the biggest contributors to his church and we expect to get our money's worth from our leadership."

As if they were three puppets controlled by one puppeteer, the three turned and marched away before Bernie could say another word. Fuming, he continued to his office. He needed to cool off before going home, but Miriam would wonder where he was. Either way she would know he was upset. He may as well go home and face the music on that score.

Nine

"Miriam, are you sure you feel well enough for me to leave you alone? You should have let Charlotte stay and help with dinner."

"I feel fine, Bernie. You know how that twenty-four hour stuff works. Knocks you down for a day then runs off to knock someone else down."

"But, Charlotte…"

"She offered to stay – even put together the salad before she left. I told her how much I appreciated her offer, but since we couldn't go out, I wanted to do something special for you. She helped me with preparations. I'll be fine. We'll dine in elegance when you get home."

"I shouldn't have to go out. This board meeting could have waited. I should have set my foot down. Why didn't I just…"

Bernie stopped mid-grumble as Miriam flashed a smile at him and moved into his arms. Sliding her arms around his neck, her lips met his. Between kisses she said, "It's all right Bernie. I would rather have our special time alone tonight anyway. It'll be nice here, just the two of us. I'll set up a table for two beside the fireplace in the parlor. We can pretend we're in some fancy New York restaurant."

"But…"

"No buts. You just go to that meeting and charm the socks off them. They need you. They're hurting."

"I know, but I'm still upset with John for sending *me* here. He knows I don't like city living. Surely someone else…"

"Bernie, you are the kindest, gentlest, most compassionate pastor John knows. You'll help these folks work through their grief."

"Someone else could have…"

"No, Bernie. A pastor they loved for over twenty years had a tragic accident. They need you."

"I'm not so sure it was an accident after what Les told me yesterday."

"Bernie, don't look for something that's not there. Mr. Jenkins might have forgotten to put the cone out and he's looking for a way to soothe his guilt. Father Jones fell down those stairs and broke his neck."

"In a church where he'd worked for over twenty years? He used those stairs several times a day." Bernie's sarcasm made his wife smile.

"Anyone can slip and fall. People do it in their homes all the time. But, I suppose you will snoop around until you're satisfied." Miriam laughed. He tried to frown, but he knew she was right. "And who knows, maybe that's why John sent you here – just to check it out, make sure it was an accident and put any rumors to rest."

"Well, Snoop *is* my name, after all," Bernie said. "When I was a kid, I came home many times with torn clothes and a bloody nose because kids made fun of me. They called me *Stupid Snoop* or sometimes *Snoopid Stoop*." Bernie cringed at the memory.

"And what did your parents say?"

Bernie smiled, still holding Miriam in his arms. "My mom begged Dad to change our name. He was adamant. It was his father's name and his grandfather's and generations before that. To change it would dishonor their memory. He said to me, 'Bernard, you can choose to be angry and fight, or you can choose to be proud and walk away. Others can't change you into their image. Only God can do that – and even God won't change you without your cooperation."

"Your father was a wise man. I wish I had known him."

"Yes, he was. He caught me snooping one Christmas. I was embarrassed and afraid he would punish me. He laughed, said it was a family trait and told me about a great-great uncle who was a famous detective. He just warned me to make sure I understood the consequences before digging into the unknown."

"Bernie…"

"I know. I'm procrastinating."

Miriam laughed and kissed him again.

"Miriam, I love you so much. Every day I thank God for you. How would I ever get along without you?"

"I love you too, darling, but God loves us even more. With his help, you'll do just fine. Now, go to that meeting before they start without you."

"Fat chance! No wonder it's called a *bored* meeting."

"Bernie!" Miriam laughed as she held his coat for him and plopped his hat on his head. She gently shoved him toward the door. He stopped, turned around and kissed her once more as if he would never have the chance to do it again.

Ten

A gust of wind carrying icy rain swept around the corner of the house. Bernie pulled his collar closer to his neck. *Not a fit night for man or beast.* He picked up his pace, smiling to himself. *That's not quite true . I love walking in all kinds of weather. Walking is good for the brain – stimulates it, clears the thoughts.*

Maybe the three-block walk would rid his mind of unkind thoughts against the board for meeting tonight when he'd told them it was his anniversary and he wanted to spend it with his wife. But here he was after ten years and he had to leave her at home alone in a new place – a city yet – on their anniversary night.

Bernie blinked as he crossed the street; he was at the church already! *Maybe this will be a short meeting. Sure, and maybe the equator is getting this freezing rain!*

*   *   *

With his back to the window listening to the sleet beat against it, Bernie sat at the conference table in the boardroom. The chatter around the table sounded like far away cowbirds gathering in a farm tree. Thoughts of farm trees led him to thoughts of the small town where he met Miriam. That led his wandering thoughts back to Miriam where he would rather be.

She's right, of course. It's too soon to skip an important meeting of the governing board of the church. But I can't understand why they wouldn't postpone this meeting until next week. It would have worked just as well and then Chuck Lewis could be here.

Chuck Lewis had been adamant. They *never* changed board meetings to satisfy personal desires. The subject was closed. Ungraciously, Bernie hoped Chuck Lewis would get a blistering sunburn while he was in California.

Bernie sighed and pulled his awareness back to the boardroom. He glanced at his watch – seven fifteen. He cleared his throat, preparing to point out the time, but Patricia Lewis, a thin anorexic-looking woman, pounded the gavel on the table. The chatter continued, so she pounded again. It was obvious to Bernie by her expression that she didn't want to be there any more than he did. She glared at him as if it Bernie was somehow the reason she had to lead the meeting.

Clearing her throat, she pounded the gavel again and raised her high-pitched, grating voice. "All right," she said, "let's get this meeting over with."

Bernie tried to pay attention. He needed to learn the ins and outs of this church. He'd already learned they leaned heavily on tradition and didn't like change or disruption. Father Jones' death had shattered their calm. The congregation, still in the clutches of grief, was angry, but their Christian faith wouldn't let them be angry with God. Less than ten minutes into the meeting, Bernie knew who would be the scapegoat for their grief.

Oh well, I have broad shoulders and a thick head. I can bear the brunt of it until they recover. Then my friend, Bishop John and I will have a long talk. This will be a short, interim pastorate – long enough to help them through their grief. Then I will move on.

Icy patters against the window distracted him as much as his own internal ramblings. He hadn't wanted to leave Oak Grove, where people were like family to him and Miriam. *Oak Grove isn't that far away – a couple hours by expressway. Ministerial ethics prevent me from returning in the role of priest, but friends can call me.* Suddenly, Bernie realized he was in his own grief process over the loss of his beloved church. He would have to work it out while helping St. Mark's with their grief.

Bernie gave himself a mental shake and once again forced his focus back to Patricia and the agenda of the evening. The usual discussions prevailed: not enough money coming in, not enough people filling the pews, not enough programs to draw in young folks, too much music, and not enough music.

With the help of supply pastors, the bishop had helped them through the Christmas season. Now, in the beginning of January, they were gearing up for Lent and finding it difficult to look forward without remembering the last twenty years. Every corner of the church had something that reminded them of Father Jones. He had been St. Mark's friend as Bernie had been a friend of St. Peter's folks. Father Jones, however, could never return – even for a short visit. Bernie sighed. He had his work cut out for him.

"What do you think, Father?"

Startled out of his musings, Bernie realized he'd missed the discussion and had no idea what Patricia was asking him.

"I'm sorry," he said, "the sleet against the window drowned out your question." Not true, but worth a try. As a matter of fact, he realized the sleet no longer badgered the window.

Patricia frowned, as did a couple of the other board members. Bernie gave them his winsome smile that usually made everything all right. Not this time, so he exchanged the smile for a philosophical win-some, lose-some shrug.

Patricia glared at him. "I *said*, I think we ought to forgo any special services for Lent this year since we are still mourning the loss of Father Jones. What do you think?"

Bernie knew he was in trouble; he could never agree to such a plan. "I think," he said rubbing his chin in thought, "that Father Jones would have been very disappointed if we ignored the services of the Christian year. Lent is vital to the theology of the church."

Voices rose and fell, each contributing at least one opinion – all at the same time. Patricia pounded the table with her husband's gavel just as Mike Ralston, the trustee chairperson, entered the room. Voices fell to a low, growling murmur.

Mike glanced around the table at his friends. "Sorry I'm late folks," he said. "I got held up at work – well not held up as in robbed – but, I didn't think you would be that upset with me for being late." Mike laughed. Several others joined him. Bernie would learn that Mike often eased the turbulence of troubled waters with his humor and easygoing ways.

"We're not complaining about *you* being late," said Paul Stone, the financial secretary. "Pat suggested that we dispense with the Lenten services this year because of Father Jones' death, but Father Snoop isn't in favor of doing that."

"Well, of course not," said Mike. "Lent is a

special time of the church year. Father Jones always said Lent was his favorite season, even more so than Christmas, because it leads to Easter. Father Jones would have been very upset if we did away with it because of him."

"Whose side are you on, anyway, Mike?" Pat glared at him.

"I didn't know we were choosing sides. Are we planning a tournament of some kind?" He followed his words with a chuckle as he pulled out an empty chair and joined them around the table. "As much as we miss our friend," he continued, "the church must move on. Even the disciples had to keep going when Jesus left them."

"He's right," said Matthew Bowman, the church treasurer. "Besides, we always use the offering from the special Lenten services to fund our mission projects. We need the Lenten services."

An hour and a half later, the meeting finally ended. Bernie reached for his coat and hat. He wanted to get out of there – get some fresh air. The sleet had stopped beating against the window, but hard to tell what was happening outside now. He was anxious to go home to Miriam.

"Come join us for coffee, Father?" Mike called to him as the group headed for the kitchen.

"Thanks, Mike, but I really need to get home."

"What's the matter, Father? Wife tightening the

apron strings?" Patricia laughed, but the sound was more bitter than joyful. "I'll have to ask her how she does it. I can't get Chuck to even come home for dinner half the time."

Bernie didn't feel he owed anyone an explanation – especially after he'd asked the board to change the meeting night for him and they refused. Putting his pique aside, he said, more to Mike than to Patricia, as the trustee helped him with his coat, "Today is our tenth anniversary. We're celebrating when I get home."

"Hey, that's great! Congratulations. Hope she's feeling well enough to celebrate."

"Thanks Mike. She's much better. Must have been that twenty-four hour flu like the doctor said."

Bernie bid them all goodnight. The sleet had turned to snow and an inch had already accumulated. Smiling to himself in spite of the cold, Bernie started walking briskly toward home. He and Miriam would snuggle before the fire and celebrate with a late candlelight dinner. He knew his beautiful, gifted wife would have prepared a special evening.

The manse was only three blocks from the church. Already Bernie missed the long walks along the quiet streets of Oak Grove, but he would eventually get used to the streets of Metropolis. Suddenly he felt that *snoopy sense* stronger than he had ever felt it. Something was wrong, but what?

He began walking faster, as if someone were chasing him. He wasn't afraid for his safety, he just felt anxious. Ever since he was a child, he had been sensitive to approaching trouble. Tonight he could almost hear the crackle – as if an electrical storm sent sparks of lightning from skyscraper to skyscraper.

He turned the corner; only another half block. *Why are lights blazing from every room in the house? Miriam is planning a candlelight dinner. The rest of the house should be dark.* A prickle of that electric current felt stronger – forced his feet to move faster. As if he had cleats on his shoes, he ran down the icy sidewalk, up the steps and across the porch. He reached for the doorknob and felt another jolt of that electric current. The door stood ajar.

"Miriam?" He called to her as he kicked the door open and ran into the entryway not bothering to stomp the snow off his feet. No answer. He called again and ran to the parlor. *She said she would set up for dinner for us in here.* He stopped in the open doorway. For a single heartbeat, time stood still.

"Miriam!" The word ended in a sob. Time moved once again, except for his beautiful wife, who lay crumpled beside the telephone stand, her sightless green eyes staring in death.

Eleven

How long Bernie stood staring at the lifeless body, he didn't know. It felt like hours, but probably was only minutes while an internal battle raged.

Pick her up. Maybe you can breathe life into her.

No, she is gone. Obviously, foul play. Don't mess up the scene.

But she needs me – I need her.

You need to call someone. Who? Neither of us has any family.

The police – you need to call the police.

But the phone is on the floor.

Finally, heaving a deep sigh that ended in a shuddered sob, Bernie stepped into the room and knelt beside Miriam's body. He had to touch her cold, lifeless face – closing her staring eyes. He let his tears flow for a few brief moments then pulled his clean handkerchief from his pocket, reached for the phone and dialed 911.

"I want…I want to report a murder," he said. Somehow he managed to keep his emotions under control while answering question and giving his address. Then he gave in to the desire to hold her.

Slipping to the floor beside her, Bernie lifted Miriam's head to his lap, caressed her face and let his tears flow.

He heard the doorbell followed by a knock and someone in the distance call out, "Police." He could not let her go in order to answer. The door was open. Voices sounded in the vestibule followed by footsteps moving toward the parlor.

"Father Snoop," a man's voice called then sounded closer. "Father Snoop, I'm Sgt. Hugh Hollohan with Metropolis Homicide. You will have to move, sir, so we can…"

A commotion in the vestibule caused the man to turn. "You can't go in there ma'am. There's been an accident."

"You and what army is going to stop me?"

Charlotte? Why is she here? She went home. Bernie squeezed his eyes closed. *Too much to understand.*

"Sorry Ma'am, but…"

"You let me in there young man or there just might be *another* accident. Father Snoop needs me."

"And who are you, Ma'am?" This came from the man who called himself Sgt. Hollohan as Charlotte pushed her way into the parlor.

"Charlotte Lane, I'm the housekeeper for the

manse. Please Sir. Let me take care of him."

"Can you get him out of here so we can work?" said the Sergeant.

"We'll be in the kitchen," she said moving close to Bernie. He felt her hands on his shoulders. "Come with me, Father," she said. "The police have to do their job. I'll make you some tea."

"Miriam…" Bernie looked into Charlotte's eyes that spilled tears down her face.

"I know, Sir. She's in God's hands now. You come with me. We'll make some tea and talk if you want to."

Bernie leaned down to kiss Miriam's face and then eased her back to the floor where he had found her. "Thank you Charlotte. Some tea might be soothing." Without another word, he stood and left the room with her.

"We'll sit in here, she said as she led him to the kitchen. She helped him remove his coat that he had forgotten he was still wearing. "I'll make you a cup of tea and put on the coffee pot in case Sgt. Hollohan and his officers want some."

Bernie sat at the table staring as if he were a blind man until Charlotte placed a mug of tea on the table before him. He wrapped his hands around the cup, letting the warmth penetrate his cold fingers wondering if his heart would ever feel warm again.

Charlotte chattered away not expecting him to

respond and simply giving him a soft background noise to chase away the internal voices that threatened to unhinge him. He was angry – with himself for leaving her alone; with the church for insisting on their stupid board meeting; with the person who had done this to her; and with God for allowing it to happen.

Charlotte sat at the table beside him. "Father Bernie, I'm so sorry. I will never forgive myself for leaving tonight. I should have insisted on staying to help. I thought she was well enough…"

Bernie realized what Charlotte was saying. She was blaming herself, believing Miriam had fallen because she was weak from the flu.

"Charlotte," said Bernie, covering her small, pudgy hand with his huge, paw of a hand. "Miriam was over the flu. She sent you home."

"But she must have still been weak."

"No. She was fine. She didn't fall because she was weak. She fell because someone knocked her down."

"But Father Bernie, that means…" Charlotte covered her mouth with her hand to hide her horror.

"Yes. Miriam was murdered."

"But…who…?"

"I have no idea. I'm sure the police will find out."

"The house does look like…maybe a burglar

thought no one was home and…"

"Maybe. We'll see what the police turn up, but don't you feel guilty."

"Nor you, Father. You had to go to that meeting. I know those folks. There'd been hell to pay if you didn't."

"Looks like there's hell to pay because I did," said Bernie.

Charlotte gasped. "Oh, Father Bernie. We'll get through this. I'm here for you in any way I can help."

"Thank you, Charlotte. Why *did* you come back?"

Charlotte managed a small smile through her tears. "My nephew is a police officer. He was there when you called. He called me. I got here about the same time they did."

"I'll never be able to thank you. I couldn't move. It was like I was dead too." Bernie took a sip of his cooling tea. "I hear someone coming. Now the questions begin."

Sergeant Hollohan opened the door from the dining room. "Would you like some coffee?" Charlotte held a cup out to him.

"Thank you," he said taking the offered cup. "Father could we talk – alone?"

"You can sit here," said Charlotte. "If it's all right, I'll use the phone in the study and make some calls to the church folks and the bishop."

"That will be fine," said Hollohan. "Now, Father Snoop, tell me what happened here tonight."

"Sergeant, I thought you might be able to tell me. I went to the board meeting at the church and when I got home I found…Miriam in the parlor."

"What time was that?"

"About nine-thirty. The meeting was over around nine-fifteen. It took me about ten minutes or so to walk."

"You walked? In this weather?"

"I like walking. It clears my mind and helps me think."

"Did you notice anything different as you approached the house?"

"Yes. Miriam had said we would have a quiet dinner by candlelight in the parlor. I wondered why all the lights were on upstairs. When I reached for the doorknob, the door was ajar."

"Then what did you do?"

"I called to Miriam, went to the parlor and found her."

"You moved her body. Did you touch anything else?"

"Sergeant Hollohan. I used my handkerchief to pick up the phone that was lying on the floor. She was my wife. I had to hold her." A sob escaped. Bernie took another gulp of air.

"Have you been through the house yet to see if

anything is missing? The officers say every room looks like someone was looking for something."

"I came from the parlor in here with Charlotte. When have I had time to look…?" Bernie stopped, realizing he was sounding sarcastic. "I'm sorry, Sergeant. I'm too numb to think clearly."

"Why don't you and Charlotte do that and let me know what you find out? In the meantime, did either you or your wife know anyone in Metropolis before coming here?"

"Only my bishop, Bishop John Murray."

"It doesn't look like any locks have been forced or windows broken. Did you lock the door?"

"Of course, we did."

"I'll talk to your housekeeper. Maybe she loaned her key to someone."

"I doubt that. I only met Charlotte two days ago, but I would trust her completely."

"Did you and your wife ever argue?"

"What is that supposed to mean? We've been married ten years. Of course we had misunderstandings–but not often and never more than a few minutes in length."

"You didn't argue tonight because she wanted you to stay home?"

"No. I wanted to stay home. She told me the church needed me."

"Did that make you angry?"

"No. Look Sergeant, I don't like where this line

of questioning is going. If you have even a tiny smidgeon of an idea that I killed my wife then you better turn in your badge and give this investigation over to someone who has more perception."

"No need to get huffy. But unless there is anything of value missing, it looks as if the *burglary* is a smoke screen – done after the fact to mislead our investigation. If it wasn't a burglar that only leaves a jealous husband, or lover."

Bernie jumped to his feet so fast the chair fell over. He stopped himself before grabbing Sergeant Hollohan around the neck. "I think you better leave Sergeant, while I'm at least partially in control of my emotions."

"And I think you better find yourself a good lawyer, Snoop. We'll talk more."

Twelve

Days blurred into weeks and weeks into months. Bernie had always been able to smile in adversity, laugh at trouble and find life exhilarating and exciting. That was *before.* Now, death had pinched out the light of his life as if someone had snuffed out a dancing candle flame. He lived in a fog of gray shadows with the exception of the Light of God's promise for comfort. Would the fog ever lift? Not until the police – or he – could stamp the case closed.

Bernie was convinced more than ever that Father Jones' death was no accident. Someone in Metropolis, and possibly his own church, was wreaking havoc on the lives of the saints in St. Mark's. Sergeant Hollohan seemed oblivious to it all. As far as he was concerned, Father Jones died from an accidental fall and Miriam at the hands of a jealous husband – or lover.

True to the expectations of April, dark clouds hung so low that pointed skyscrapers pricked their bellies sending a misty fog into the gray twilight of evening. Spring was several weeks' old and warm days had brought green lawns and budding trees, but the gray chill of this April day suggested the possibility of snow.

Bernie had always enjoyed walking to clear his mind, but today he shuffled aimlessly, crossing one street then another, paying no attention to his direction. He shivered when the wind-swept mist invaded his open coat, sending icy fingers to massage neck and shoulder muscles tense with grief, frustration and anger. He gripped the wool collar and pulled it closer to him.

Even though the Lenten season had come and gone and Bernie hardly remembered it, for the first time in his ministry, Bernie really understood the meaning of Lent, the suffering of his Lord. Easter was a blur.

Where is the hope of Easter? Sure, I believe in the resurrection, but like Mary and Martha at the death of their beloved brother, Lazarus, I need comfort now – in the present. How can I live without Miriam?

Suddenly, as if answering his questions from beyond the grave, Miriam's words came back to him, played around his consciousness and pricked his sense of guilt for not having complete trust in God.

"God loves us more than we love each other," she'd said. "With God's help, you'll do just fine."

But will I? Of course, I will. I lived alone most of my life until…

Had Charlotte not been there, forcing him to eat, to talk, to live, he wasn't sure where he would be. In spite of his funky mood, a small smile tugged at the corners of his mouth. *That woman is like a drill sergeant, but it's what I needed. I'm glad she was smart enough to know that.*

Bernie heard an almost coughing sound behind him. He stopped walking and listened. Looking around him, he realized he was in unfamiliar surroundings. There was that sound again.

"Yap, yap, yap!"

He turned around and saw a shaggy white something – dog he presumed, or large cat. It looked like an automated dust mop chasing behind him, sweeping the sidewalk as it ran.

"I don't remember seeing you before," said Bernie. "Come to think about it, I don't remember this neighborhood, either."

The little dog snapped at his heels. When Bernie didn't move, it sat at his feet and looked up at him as if to say, "Didn't I scare you even a little bit?"

Before Bernie could say anything more to the little dog, someone opened a door somewhere .A man's deep voice called out, "Brutus! Get in here you stupid mutt!"

The dog gave one last yap at Bernie then scampered away to the man. The door closed with a finality that said, "You know better than to talk to strangers."

Bernie stared after the dog. *Brutus?* Again, a smile played at the corner of his mouth. *Such a ridiculous name for a scrappy little dust mop of a dog. Miriam would have thought the dog a beautiful animal.*

Not ready to give up his mournful mood, Bernie forced his face back to its melancholy mask and plunged his hands deep within his pockets. He plodded on, looking for a sign that would tell him where he was. Nothing looked familiar and yet at the same time looked like almost any neighborhood – row after row of houses that looked so nearly alike that he wondered if people ever entered the wrong door. Glancing at the skyline, he walked in the direction of downtown.

Thoughts of Sergeant Hollohan and the investigation took every opportunity to invade his thinking. Bernie didn't attempt to exorcise such disturbing thoughts. *Someone has to give the murder its proper time in thought and logic.*

"Hollohan is a bumbling idiot. It's been over three months. He should have something by now." Bernie mumbled to himself, but deep inside he could almost hear Miriam chiding him, "Now, Bernie, the man's doing the best he can."

"Then why hasn't he found the culprit?" Words

intended for his inner ear only, sounded loud and harsh.

A man walking his dog, turned. "You talking to me, mister?"

Shaking his head and shoving his hands deeper into his pockets, Bernie crossed the street. He didn't want to get into a discussion with a stranger.

As he continued to walk, he picked up his thoughts about Hollohan. *The man seems to have a one-track mind when it comes to murder – at least to Miriam's murder. He still believes that either I killed her in a quarrel, or she had a lover on the side that killed her in a quarrel. At least he was smart enough to realize there was no burglary. Someone tried to make it look that way. Nothing of importance was missing. There was no evidence of a break-in. Someone had a key or else Miriam admitted the killer into the house. Either way, it came back to the same conclusion. She knew her killer. But we'd been in town less than forty-eight hours. She hadn't even met folks at our church that first Sunday because she stayed home with the flu.*

Bernie pulled his hands from his pocket and pressed his temples. Nothing made sense. He'd give Hollohan another call Monday. But now it was getting late and he needed to get to the church and go over his message for tomorrow. *If only I could drag myself out of this fog – literal and mental. I've always been good at solving puzzles of any kind. So why does the answer to this one evaded me?*

The April drizzle began to accumulate on Bernie's hat and drip to his shoulders. He pulled his collar around his neck again and thrust his hands back into his pockets. Back in familiar territory, he stopped at the corner of Market and Main and stared into the gathering darkness. Streetlights gave off a yellowish glow; storefronts added their display lights; still the gloom gathered as if some light-eating dragon had descended and gobbled up all existing rays from the street lamps.

I should go home, but for what reason? Miriam won't be there to greet me. Even if Charlotte were there, which she's not, she's bossier than my own mother ever was. No, I'll go to the church. I love the silence of an empty church because God has always met me there. No one ever comes to the church on Saturday night –unless we're having a wedding or special meeting.

Most folks at St. Mark's, because of their own grief, understood Bernie's loss and tried to be consoling. Others, however, still blamed him – no matter how irrationally – for their loss of Father Jones. Some even went so far as to insinuate that Miriam's death was punishment for his crime of replacing the good Father. Some wanted him to leave, but Sergeant Hollohan suggested very strongly that he not leave town until they solved the murder. As if he would ever leave before he saw the killer behind bars! He sighed and turned down Long Street toward the church.

The one hundred and fifty year old structure stood like a dark giant against the gray sky. He climbed the stone stairs to the front door rather than walk around to the back alley entrance to his office.

The giant double doors with stained glass in the upper third, pulled open easily. *Les keeps the hinges well oiled.* The doors closed with a soft *thunk* leaving the entryway in darkness except for the spots of color where the streetlights sifted through stained glass. Bernie knew the way to the sanctuary, so he didn't bother to turn on a light. *Besides, if the light is on, it might encourage passers-by to stop and chat. I don't want any chatter tonight.*

Entering the narthex, he made his way to a back pew of the sanctuary. Except for the normal creaks and groans of an old building, it was so quiet Bernie could hear his heartbeat. He removed his hat and sat quietly inviting the *still small voice* to soothe his aching heart.

Sometime later, feeling somewhat comforted, Bernie rose and with head bowed and shoulders hunched, shuffled to the end of the hall. Light filtered through rain-streaked, stained glass windows from the street lamps and parking lots. He continued down the dark corridor to the right, past the secretary's office and choir room to his office. Closing the door behind him, Bernie reluctantly lit the desk lamp. He preferred the darkness, but needed light to work. Pitching his coat and hat to the hall tree that stood by the alley door, he took a deep breath, eased himself onto his swivel chair and gave it a couple of turns. Finally, he rested his elbows on the walnut desk surface – far too extravagant a desk as far as he was concerned – and turned on the computer.

Miriam had insisted that he learn to use the computer and he was glad she did. His thoughts came in spurts these days and it was easier to save them on a computer than written notes that got lost. While he waited for the system to go through its start-up routine, he rocked from side to side in the chair, his thoughts whirling like the rain now beating against the windows.

Like a dog gnawing on an old bone, Bernie kept returning to the same old, unanswered questions. *The police are doing nothing – at least as far as I can tell. They watch me as if waiting for me to crack and run to them with a confession. It looks like I'll have to look more seriously into the matter myself.*

Living up to his name, Bernie had already been snooping into some areas that he thought more likely than Hollohan did. *The police have their pet theories – a stranger looking for a handout, committed the crime; Miriam had a lover on the side; or I killed her. I know Miriam would never have allowed a stranger into our home while I was gone, especially not in a home where we had lived less than forty-eight hours. And a lover? That's preposterous! And, of course, I know I didn't kill her.*

The murderer has to be either someone she knew, and/or someone who had a key to our home. That is a scary thought, because it means someone from St. Mark's killed her. That's as impossible to believe as the idea of Miriam having a lover. And yet…how many people have a key to the manse?

Bernie pulled the file from his desk drawer. Even though he had committed the names to memory, he checked the notes he'd written: Mike Ralston had one as trustee chair; the Manse Committee chairperson had one, and Charlotte had one.

Mike was at the board meeting that night, as was Mona Hunt, the Manse Committee chairperson. Charlotte had gone home early because Miriam wanted to fix their anniversary dinner herself. Mike was late for the meeting, but Hollohan had checked his alibi. He was at work as he said he was.

A sound outside the window brought Bernie out of his reverie. How long he'd brooded he didn't know, but the screensaver fish swam back and forth across the monitor as if it were a lighted aquarium. Rain continued to blow against the storm windows, which rattled in the howling wind, but he was sure he heard someone, or something, crying.

"Is someone out there?" he called out.

There was no answer.

Maybe I was mistaken. If someone is out there, he would have knocked on my door. Maybe they did and I didn't hear?

Bernie got up, stretched and moved toward the windows. He raised one and peered into the dark alley. He saw only streams of water running down the storm window. Suddenly he smelled smoke.

"That's coming from inside," he said to himself. "The kitchen?"

He jerked around and went to the inside door that led to downstairs. A gray curling cloud crept under the door, pulling itself inward and upward like a genie released from its lamp. It filled the room, swallowing up necessary oxygen.

"Holy Smoke," said Bernie reaching for the phone with one hand and the computer with the other. "The church is on fire!"

Thirteen

The phone was dead. As if that gray genie had closed its giant fist around the electrical system, pinching the surge like a candlewick flame, the room plunged into darkness.

Bernie grabbed his coat and hat and by feel tried the alley door while pushing his arms into the coat sleeves. The door wouldn't budge. He pushed harder. Still nothing. *It feels like something is stuck against it. Better try the window.* Smoke surrounded him, stinging his eyes and nose, sending tears streaming down his face. Pulling a handkerchief from his pocket, he covered his mouth and nose.

"The window I opened is left of the door." Bernie talked to himself to chase away the panic that was rising and to keep disorientation at a minimum. Feeling his way along the shelf, he reached the still open window.

Running his hand over the smooth glass storm window, he tried to find a way to open it. "It's stuck like the door. Is someone trying to trap me in here?"

Anger mixed with adrenaline gave power to his muscles. Determination sent his hand to the remembered bookend on the shelf between the door and window. Clutching it firmly in a gloved hand, he smacked the window. The bookend bounced back hitting his shoulder, sending a clang echoing around the room. Bernie hit it again – harder. Finally, the windowpane shattered sending a spray of glass particles to the floor and to the alley outside. Icy fingers of rain slapped against his face, but Bernie hardly noticed as he leaned out gulping in great swallows of air.

I need to get out of here. He covered his face with his arm and broke the remaining glass from the edges of the window. Then he climbed out and dropped to the alley below. Sirens wailed in the distance, moving closer. *Someone must have seen the smoke and called for help.*

Collar up, hat pulled down, Bernie ducked his head against the blowing wind and rain as he continued to take deep breaths. He heard the same cry that he'd heard earlier near the window. This time it came from the ground near his feet. His eyes adjusting to the twilight darkness of the alley, he saw something move by his ankle. Stooping, he saw a wet slimy something that could have been either a very large rat or a very small cat. Whatever was there, it was soaked, shivering and crying as it brushed against his fingers.

Heedless of possible sharp teeth, Bernie picked the creature up, held it in his cupped hands and carried it to the corner of the building where light from the parking lot reflected against puddles. It was a kitten as grey as the twilight and as soaked as a fish in a pond. It stared at him then mewed softly almost pleadingly.

"Well, where did you come from?" Bernie asked, not expecting an answer. "You can't be more than a few months old." The kitten shivered, opened its mouth and licked Bernie's fingers. "Poor little fellow, you're soaked and probably starved. Let's get you warm and dry then we'll find something for you to eat in a little bit. You probably saved my life tonight. I could have been overcome by the smoke in there."

The kitten, a scrawny animal with wet fur clinging to its bones, snuggled against Bernie and began to purr. For the first time since Miriam's death, Bernie felt a genuine smile of pleasure. "Holy Smoke. That's what I'll call you."

While Bernie had been talking to the kitten, sirens had stopped wailing and the reflection of red lights flashed from the front of the church. He placed the kitten in a deep inside pocket of his coat next to his chest. "You'll be nice and warm in there until I can get you home."

"Hey, you. What are you doing back here?"

Someone called to him from the end of the alley. Bernie moved toward the firefighter running toward him.

"I'm Father Bernard Snoop, the pastor of this church. I was working late in my office. Smoke started rolling under one of my doors. The alley door was stuck so I broke the window to get out. The kitchen is under my office. Could be coming from down there."

While Bernie explained, he and the firefighter walked back down the alley to the door to his office. The firefighter turned his flashlight on the door. "No wonder you couldn't get out the door. Looks like someone jammed it with a two by four. Better leave it for the police. Is there another way in back here?"

"Why would anyone…? Never mind. You might want to try the front entrance or the stairs over on 32nd Street. They lead to the fellowship hall and the kitchen," said Snoop.

"You the one who called it in?"

"No. I tried by my office phone was dead."

"Did you see or hear anyone?" The firefighter continued to run the beam of light over the side of the building. Phone wires dangled in two pieces. "Looks like someone cut them."

Bernie shook his head in disbelief. *What is going on?*

"When I'm in the office with the doors closed, sounds are pretty well blocked out. No one ever comes to the church on Saturday night unless we have a meeting. I did hear a noise outside a window. It turned out to be a kitten on the windowsill. That's when I noticed the smoke."

"Why are you here so late?"

"I often stop by on Saturday nights to think and pray and put finishing touches on my message for Sunday."

Bernie walked with the firefighter to the side of the building. "This is the entrance to downstairs," he said pulling out a ring of keys.

"Stick around. The police will want your statement."

"I'm sure they will."

The firefighter gave him a curious look, but started down the stairs and Bernie continued around to the front of the building to wait. Even though this was a fire, not murder, he was sure Hollohan would find some reason to show up.

Although Bernie saw no flames, black smoke continued to roll from open doors. Maybe it's all smoke and no fire. A chill ran down his spine. *Was that the intent? Death by smoke inhalation?* The wind shifted and he caught the definitive odor of gasoline, or some kind of chemical. *This fire was no accident.*

"Father Bernie, what's going on here?" Paul

Stone, financial chairperson, called to him as he ran across the street. "I was driving by and saw the smoke and fire trucks. You just get here?"

"No, I was in my office," said Bernie, "but, I was aware of nothing until smoke started rolling under my door. My phone was dead so I couldn't call out. The alley door was stuck. I grabbed my coat and went out a window. Apparently someone else saw the smoke and called for help."

"You were sure lucky," said Paul "Looks like one of the ladies left a burner on again. We've all told them repeatedly about double checking."

"So have I," said Bernie. He decided to say nothing about his unsettling thoughts. Let the authorities take care of it. If it were arson and attempted murder, they would know.

"We just paid our premium on the church insurance," said Paul, always thinking like a financial person. "We should be in good shape. Maybe they'll put out the fire before it reaches the sanctuary."

"I certainly hope so," said Bernie. "We may have to cancel church tomorrow, but…"

"Father Snoop!" A young man ran toward him.

"Tim," said Bernie, reaching out a hand to grasp the younger man's hand.

"What happened?"

"We don't know yet," said Bernie. "I was just

telling Paul we'll have to cancel church in the morning – no fire, but lots of smoke damage."

Bernie turned to his financial secretary. "Paul, I believe you've met Reverend Speers, pastor of the Baptist Church across the street."

"We've met." Paul nodded, but didn't offer to shake hands.

"Our worship service is at nine o'clock and Sunday School meets downstairs at ten. Your service is at eleven, why don't you use our sanctuary until you get settled?"

"Tim, I appreciate that. I'll call the radio station and have it announced tonight as well as first thing in the morning. I'll come over early and put a sign out front."

"I don't know, Father," said Paul. "Chuck won't like it if we make a big decision like that without his knowledge. Some of our folks won't like meeting in a different place – especially a Baptist church." He smiled at Reverend Speers, who shrugged and started to walk away.

"Thanks for your offer, Tim," Bernie called after him. "We'll take you up on it." Tim smiled and waved as he ran back down the street.

Bernie turned back to Paul. "This is an emergency and there isn't time to call a board meeting. Chuck is probably out of town anyway. I'm sure most of our folks will appreciate having a place to worship."

"You're asking for more trouble," said Paul. "You know how stubborn Chuck is."

"We can't refuse an offer made in love. We have to meet somewhere. It's going to take weeks, if not longer, to clean up this mess."

"Maybe we should just close the church and forget it." Paul rammed his hands in his pockets and hunched against the rain. "Some folks been talking about it anyway."

Father Snoop gave him a sharp look. "You too, Paul? I know there are some who want to close the church, or get rid of me. Is that what you're saying? That I should leave and everything will return to normal?"

"I didn't say that, Father."

"You didn't have to. I'll call the radio stations from home." Without waiting for Paul to answer, Bernie turned and walked away. *If the police want to talk to me, they know where to find me.*

The three blocks home didn't give Bernie near enough time to clear his mind of the uneasiness and anger that boiled within him. *That fire was set deliberately and the door blocked to either kill me or give the church reason to remove me.* He felt movement next to his heart. "Holy Smoke," he said and smiled as he started up his walk.

Inside the house, he removed the cat from his pocket. Almost dry, he was still a smoke-gray color with beautiful, blue eyes. *Like a Siamese.* He set the kitten on the floor and turned to the refrigerator. "Why don't you explore the kitchen a little while I warm some milk for you?"

The kitten took a few tentative steps across the slippery, linoleum floor. Bernie poured a small amount of milk in a saucer and put it in the microwave just long enough to warm it. Then he set it on the floor. "Come on, Smoke," he said. "It's yours. Come and eat it."

Holy Smoke looked at Bernie then at the dish, then padded over and began lapping it up. Bernie smiled and reached for the phone to call the local radio and TV stations.

After he had made the last call, he picked the kitten up and holding it close to his face, he said, "Holy Smoke, after church tomorrow we'll go to the store to buy you some food and..." He stopped suddenly struck by reality.

"But you need a litter box tonight, don't you? And more than a small saucer of milk to eat. All right, let's go see what we can find." He placed the cat back in his pocket and went to the garage for the car. Not far from his street was a strip mall. He was sure he had seen a Pet Store there. He hoped they were open. Lights were still on when he parked the car. Keeping Smoke in his inside pocket, he went in and bought everything he thought a cat would need – food, dishes, litter box and filler and of course toys. He was smiling as he drove home. Even seeing Hollohan's car in his driveway didn't dull his newfound joy.

Bernie pulled his Volkswagen around Hollohan's Ford and drove into his garage. Hollohan walked toward him as he got out of the car.

"You always go shopping so late at night?"

"Not always," answered Bernie.

"Why'd you leave the scene?"

Bernie nodded toward the door to the kitchen. "It's warmer inside if this is going to be a long visit. Shall I make coffee? I think Charlotte made a chocolate cake."

"This isn't a social call, Snoop."

"No, I didn't think so, but we can still talk inside where it's warmer. I have things to do."

Bernie gathered his purchases from the car and stepped into the kitchen, leaving the door open for Hollohan, who followed him in. Bernie set his purchases on the table and removed the kitten from his inside coat pocket.

"What is that?" Hollohan stared at the gray rat-like creature. Holy Smoke stared back with blue piercing eyes."

Bernie chuckled. "This is Holy Smoke," he said stroking the kitten's head. "He saved my life tonight."

"Saved your life?"

"Well, in a manner of speaking." Bernie then told him about going to the office, the kitten crying outside his window, the smoke rolling into the room and his breaking the window to get out.

"You didn't see or hear anything else?"

"No, but now that I think back, the smoke rolled into my office too fast to be creeping under the door. It actually blew across the room as if an open door caused a sudden draft."

"You didn't try to go out the door?"

"I tried the alley door. It was stuck. By then the room was full of smoke. The electricity was off. My eyes were burning. I couldn't see anything. I felt my way back to the window and broke it with something from the bookshelf."

"You could have set the fire yourself and broke the window to…"

"You're grabbing at straws, Sergeant. Someone tried to kill me tonight whether you believe it or not. And I would be willing to bet it's the same person who killed my wife…and Father Jones."

"Jones was an accident. Why you?"

"Because I don't believe Father Jones died by accident. I believe someone in this town – possibly my own church – killed him as well as Miriam. He knows I won't stop snooping until he's behind bars."

"You're asking for trouble, Snoop."

"Only if I'm right."

Hollohan stared at him for a moment, pocketed his notebook and left.

"Smoke," said Bernie, "I think I'm finally getting through to him."

*   *   *

Bernie had finished putting Holy Smoke's things away. He threw a fuzzy mouse across the floor and Smoke ran after it and pounced just as the back door opened. Bernie looked up surprised.

"Charlotte! Did you forget something?"

"No, Father. I heard the news about the church and I came to see if you're all right. They said someone was in the building."

"I was, but my little friend here saved my life."

"Friend?" Charlotte glanced down at the gray statue with blue eyes.

Bernie laughed. Charlotte raised her eyebrows. "I don't think I've ever heard you laugh, Father. It sounds wonderful."

"It's all his fault," said Bernie. "Charlotte, meet Holy Smoke. Smoke, this is Charlotte, who takes care of me. If you're nice to her, she might take care of you too."

Holy Smoke blinked then walked over and rubbed against Charlotte's ankles.

"I hope you aren't allergic to cats," said Bernie.

"Not at all. And if this little fellow saved your

life, I'll treat him like royalty. What happened?"

"Pull up a chair, Charlotte. I was just going to have a cup of tea and a piece of your chocolate cake. Why don't you join me and I'll tell you everything that happened tonight."

Charlotte poured the tea while Bernie sliced the cake. They sat at the table and Bernie filled her in on the night's happenings. When Charlotte left a half-hour later, she was already on good terms with Holy Smoke and one of the few people who would ever know the complete story of the church fire, as well as Bernie's suspicions.

Fourteen

April slipped into May and May to June. Bernie with Smoke draped around his shoulder like a prayer shawl, stopped to talk with the workers in the sanctuary. The walls sparkled in the late afternoon sunlight.

"That's a perfect shade of blue," said Bernie as the painter stopped to rest a minute.

"It does look nice with the colors in the stained glass," he said. "We should finish the paint today or early tomorrow. I understand the carpet layers want to start tomorrow."

"Only if you're done," said Bernie. "Take your time. It's been decades since we did anything in here and will probably be decades longer before we do it again. We want it done right."

"That's our motto, Father – A job worth doing is worth doing right."

"Meow!" Smoke added his comment. The painter looked surprised then laughed.

"I think he agrees," said Bernie as he started toward the corridor where the offices were. He stopped to see Alice before going to his office.

"It's looking good out there, Father," she said. "Maybe the fire was a blessing in disguise."

"Maybe."

"I'm sure glad they did this section first. It's nice to work in a new, clean office with equipment that works."

"Most of the damages were in this section – your office, the choir room, the boardroom and my office," said Bernie.

"I know you had a lot to do with getting the improvements done," she said. "Thanks for standing up to the trustees. I'm sure they weren't too easily persuaded that the offices and choir room needed to be done first."

Bernie grimaced then smiled. "You might say that," he said remembering the three-hour discussion that led to the priority list of renovations.

"Barring any unforeseen catastrophes we should be able to worship here Sunday. Would you write a thank you letter to Reverend Speers and the Baptist congregation? Tom Jenkins is supposed to drop off a check from the church to send with it."

Alice laughed. "I heard through the grapevine about the meeting last night. Again, Father Bernie, thank you for sticking to your guns and making them do what is right."

"Well," said Bernie, "the Baptists have been more than kind to us these last two months. We can't just walk away with no word of thanks."

Bernie picked up the pink message slips and started back to his office. Nothing from Hollohan.

Bernie sat at his desk and turned on the computer. Smoke chased a toy around the room for a while then jumped to the shelf where Bernie kept a flat pillow for him. He soon curled into a ball, napping until time to go home.

Bernie pulled several file folders from his briefcase and opened them. Logging on to the internet, he did some research oblivious of the time until Alice knocked at his door, then opened it.

"It's almost five, Father," she said. "Do you need for me to stay over?"

"Is it that late already? Thanks, Alice, but I'm just going to work a while longer then head home. You can lock up on your way out. I'll go out the alley door."

Bernie ran his *snoopy findings* though his mind while he turned pages in the first folder. *The key seems to be the key factor – no pun intended. I've double-checked all the people who were supposed to have keys and those who actually have them. Some loaned theirs to relatives, some duplicated to replace lost keys and some are simply unaccounted for. It seems that everyone who has a key to the church also has a key to the manse. Maybe I should change the locks and see who yells first.*

Bernie was startled when the corridor door suddenly flew open and banged against the wall. Smoke, who had been sleeping on his pillow on the bookshelf, leaped to the corner of Bernie's desk – fur standing on end, back arched.

Chuck Lewis slammed the door behind him and strode over to Bernie's desk. Placing his hands on the desk, he leaned toward Bernie. The scowl told Bernie Chuck was not happy – even if the banging door hadn't. Chuck had missed the meeting last night because of one of his many out of town business trips.

"Father *Snoop*," he sneered the name and glared at Bernie. "I thought I made it clear that *no* important business was to be discussed without me being present. What was the idea of calling a board meeting last night when you knew I was out of town?"

"I did not call a special meeting. It was the regular night for the board."

"I specifically left word that I would be out of town and the meeting had to be changed."

"You also made it very clear back in January that the board meeting night is *never* changed for personal reasons."

"I've warned you enough. Who gave you the right to authorize the treasurer to pay the Baptists for use of their building? They offered it. No cost was mentioned."

"It was not payment. We could never pay them what we should. It was simply a token gift of thanks for the use of the building and for their hospitality."

"And you are still snooping around, harassing people about keys. People are getting tired of you asking repeatedly for them to account for their keys and tell *you* when they were last used. It is none of your business…"

Bernie broke in. "I beg to differ with you Mr. Lewis. The only keys I'm interested in are those that fit the house in which I live. I have every right to know who has access to my home."

"It's not *your* home. That house belongs to us – the church."

"As long as I live in it, it is my home."

"You have been nothing but trouble ever since you came here, Snoop. I want you to stop snooping into things that don't concern you – now. I want you to back off and leave us alone. Is that understood?"

"You have no power or right to give me orders, Lewis. Miriam's death makes it all my concern and my business," said Bernie, looking him in the eye. "I will back off as soon as Miriam's murderer is behind bars."

"You'll find yourself behind bars," shouted Chuck. "We're getting tired of your snooping and accusations. There are laws against harassment."

Bernie turned off the computer, put the folders in his briefcase and stood. Smoke jumped to his shoulder. Bernie opened the alley door and walked away, before he said more than was prudent. He left Chuck Lewis staring, shooting imaginary daggers after him

Bernie walked home, letting the mild June air soothe him. He was tired – hadn't been home since noon. He smiled remembering the lunch Charlotte had prepared for him. His mind on other things, he had started to leave without eating. Charlotte stood with her back against the door, hands on hip and head tilted back to look up into his face.

"Father Bernie," she'd said, "you have to pay more attention to eating. Look at you. You are just a pile of bones held together with that tough stubborn hide. Even Holy Smoke eats better than you do."

Bernie had smiled at her, thanked her for caring and forced himself to eat the lunch she prepared. Now it was almost eight o'clock. The aroma of vegetable lasagna met him as he opened the door and he smiled again. He would have to reheat it – or not. It was good either way. Charlotte grumbled, but she took good care of him.

Before he could even close the door behind him, the phone began ringing. Smoke jumped to the telephone stand and sniffed at the phone, one paw ready to step on the speakerphone button.

Bernie laughed, a feeling he was enjoying more and more with Holy Smoke around. "Go ahead," he said, "punch the button. You're as curious as I am – or is it the other way around?"

Smoke pressed the button and said, "Meow."

"What? Who is that? Bernie is that you trying to be funny?"

Bernie laughed again. "No, John, not me. That was Holy Smoke, my cat. He was going to take a message. How are you?"

"Bernie, when did you get a cat? You never… Never mind. I need to talk to you."

"So, talk. No one here but Smoke and he's trustworthy – more than some people I know." Bernie ran his hand down Smoke's sleek, gray back while he talked to his friend, Bishop John Murray.

"I don't want to talk on the phone."

"All right. How about lunch? We still haven't had that long leisurely lunch you mentioned when you asked me to come to Metropolis."

"That's tempting, Bernie, but not this time. Can you come to my office? Say tomorrow? Nine o'clock?"

"Is this an order, or a request?"

"Bernie, we've been friends too long…"

"Not a problem, John. I'll be there."

"Good. Nine o'clock."

"Sure," Bernie answered, but was talking to a buzzing dial tone. "Smoke, looks like I've really shook up the troops. Chuck must have called a caucus and gave John a call almost as soon as I left the church."

Bernie chuckled and picked up Holy Smoke, who butted his head against Bernie's jaw and purred. Bernie carried Smoke to the kitchen to heat his lasagna and get a bedtime snack for the cat.

Fifteen

Father Snoop pulled his VW into spot # 3 in the parking deck attached to Bishop Murray's downtown office building – the same spot that he and Miriam used last December. He sat for a minute or two staring across the Metropolis skyline. He hadn't been to John's office since then. For that matter, he hadn't seen John to talk to him since the funeral. And even then, John was too busy to talk.

"You know, Smoke," he said to his faithful companion in the passenger seat, "when John asked me to come to Metropolis, he said, and I quote, 'It will be good to have you nearby, Bernie. We can get together often for lunch just to reminisce.' That was in December. Except for Miriam's funeral, I've seen him three times – all business occasions."

Bernie reached across the passenger seat to stroke the cat, which had grown from a skinny, soaked rat-shaped animal to a sleek, regal feline in the past three months. "Smoke," he said, "I don't have a good feeling about this meeting." Holy Smoke nudged Bernie's elbow and purred.

"John Murray and I have been friends since our first day at seminary. Other students called us *Mutt and Jeff*." Snoop chuckled at the memory. "We were as different as night and day – except where our faith and calling were concerned. He officiated at my wedding." Bernie was silent for a moment then spoke in a soft almost reverent tone, "Six months and no word."

Bernie shook his head and opened the car door. "Well, I suppose we won't know what he wants unless we go see. He said nine o'clock. Sounded a bit formal for John. Bound to mean trouble."

Bernie unfolded his six-foot frame from the VW. Smoke leapt to his shoulder. Bernie walked with what he hoped looked like a confident stride into the building, took the elevator to the twenty-second floor that opened into the lobby of Bishop Murray's office. Nothing had changed – the same gold speckled carpet, gold draperies and wall of windows. The only difference was that two Monet summer scenes had replaced the Currier and Ives winter scenes.

"Good morning, Father Bernie," said Clarice. "Who's your friend?" She smiled and reached to let Smoke sniff her fingers.

Bernie returned her smile. "This is Holy Smoke."

Clarice laughed. "An appropriate name with his gray color."

"More than you know," said Bernie. He didn't bother to explain the events leading to the cat's name.

"The bishop is waiting for you," she said nodding toward the closed door – the room they jokingly referred to as *The Oval Office.* "Go on in."

"Thank you," said Bernie then taking a deep breath reached for the door. As he opened it, John stood and stretched his arm across the wide, expensive walnut desk to shake hands. "Bernie! Welcome, welcome. Come in. Come in." A broad smile spread across his round face – a smile too broad and a greeting too exuberant. "Good to see you."

"John," said Bernie taking his hand. "Or is it *Bishop* today?"

Instead of answering, the bishop called to his secretary. "Clarice, would you bring us something to drink?" Turning back to Bernie, he asked, "Ice tea? Coffee? Something stronger?"

"Nothing for me, thanks," said Bernie. Smoke jumped from his shoulder as Bernie eased into the gray wing-tipped leather chair across the desk from the bishop. "I've had my morning coffee," said Bernie, "and nine o'clock is a little early for anything stronger – even if I were so inclined. Or, is this a test? Afraid I've become an alcoholic?"

"I know you better than that, Bernie, but how

are you coping?" A serious expression replaced the artificial smile.

Ignoring his question, Bernie turned to Smoke, who made himself comfortable on the arm of the leather chair, folding his front paws under him and squeezing his eyes shut. "I don't think you've met my new companion," he said. "This is Holy Smoke. He answered the phone last night. A few months back, he saved my life. He often accompanies me places. Hope you don't mind."

Bernie smiled to himself as he watched Bishop Murray cringe. He knew Smoke wouldn't dig his claws into the chair, but he didn't bother to tell his friend. Let him stew. John mumbled something that sounded like, "Course not, but you didn't answer my question."

"Come on, John, what's up. We've been friends a long time. You didn't ask me to your office just for coffee or inquire about my health. What's on your mind?"

"Bernie, you look tired – almost haggard. When did you last have a vacation?"

"I haven't even been at St. Mark's six months. Why would I need a vacation? What are you getting at—a forced vacation? Leave of absence? Sabbatical? Maybe a year or so without a church?"

"Bernie…"

"Which is it, *Bishop?* You have some reason for calling me in for a nine o'clock meeting – after a short, heated argument with my Senior Warden, I might add." Bernie leaned forward on the edge of his chair. Smoke kept his eyes closed, but his ears twitched.

"I just thought you ought to consider a six month sabbatical. It would do you a world of good." Bishop Murray pulled his white linen handkerchief from his pocket and mopped at his brow.

"I don't need a sabbatical. Are you telling me you want me out of the church?"

"Well, you haven't been yourself since you lost your wife in that terrible accident..."

"John, I did not *lose* my wife. If we truly believe in the afterlife that we preach, I know exactly where she is. And it wasn't an accident. She was murdered. But how would you know how I've been? I haven't seen you since the funeral – except in passing at a couple of business meetings."

"Bernie...it's been almost a year now. Don't you think you should begin to get over your grief – stop...?"

"It's been less than six months, not a year. But, let me ask you something – as a friend – John. I know why as a bishop you put the pressure on Hollohan to call it an accident. You needed to prevent a scandal in the church. But, as a friend, how can you ignore the facts?"

"Bernie, the facts are in the report in my file. Miriam was feverish; she got up and fell, breaking her neck – probably tripped over that cat."

Bernie clamped his jaws together, balled his hands into fists and took a deep breath. Slowly he blew out the *bad* air and with it the *bad* thoughts. He replied with much more calm than he felt. "Holy Smoke wasn't even around at the time. Miriam was not ill, except for that twenty-four hour flu which lasted until Sunday afternoon. That might be the report you have, but Hollohan's is very different. I am still the number one suspect in her death – as well as the fire three months ago – and was told not to leave town until her murder is solved."

"Bernie, she tripped."

"John, I found her. She had a handprint on her face. Someone slapped her and knocked her down. She hit her head on the table."

"There were no fingerprints except yours and hers."

"Do you think she slapped herself and then threw her body to the floor? Come on John, I thought you were my friend."

"Bernie, if it was murder why aren't the police...?"

"Because *you* stopped them. Either because you believe I killed her, or to keep a scandal out of the church, or both."

"Bernie…"

"That's it, isn't it? You believe I killed my wife. Well I didn't and I'm not leaving town until *I* find her killer. You can remove me from the church. You can set my furniture on the sidewalk to make room for another priest, but you cannot make me leave town."

"Bernie…"

"Good day, *Bishop*. I have work to do." Bernie stood, Smoke leapt to his shoulder.

"Bernie, wait. You're right; we've been friends too long to part this way." Bishop Murray wiped the perspiration from his brow again. The air conditioner suddenly kicked on, humming quietly at the window. Bernie stopped, half turned and waited.

"I couldn't believe it when that policeman – Hollohan – told me what he believed, but like you said it's my job to protect the church. They're asking me to relieve you of your duties."

"They? Who are they? The police, or the church?"

"The personnel committee at St. Mark's."

"I'll find a room somewhere…" Once again, Bernie started for the door.

"Wait, Bernie. Maybe we can work out a compromise."

"Compromise?"

"I have a young priest who needs a church as part of his schooling – student intern. He could be your associate. He's single, no family. He can live with you and take as much responsibility as you and the church find necessary. I'll tell the committee that he's there to assess your mental and spiritual health for us, since we can't remove you without documented cause."

"And will he? And will you?"

"Of course not, but...unless you've changed in recent years, I know you're living up to your name. If you have someone to accept the responsibilities of the church, you will be free to snoop all you want. When the murderer is behind bars, we'll find you a church somewhere and you can start over. Then the young priest can take over full responsibility."

"John, it sounds great, but..."

"But what?"

"As you say, I have already been snooping. Holy Smoke helps. After the church fire, the police found bundles of tarp and rags soaked in kerosene smoldering by the stairwell near my office. A fan blew smoke toward my office. Whoever set the fire never intended to burn the church. They blocked the corridor and outside doors to trap me. John, I'm convinced someone in the church killed both Father Jones and Miriam and has tried to kill me. I'm almost certain who, but I don't know why and I can't prove it – yet. I don't want you to put a young man in danger."

"Bernie, if you ever feel the young man is in danger, call me. I'll pull him immediately."

"All right. Does this young priest have a name?"

"He's a student at our seminary. His name is David Suiter. Very nice young man."

Bernie smiled and Bishop Murray arched his eyebrows. "You know him?"

"There was a kid in my first parish with that name. Maybe not the same person. If it is, he *is* a nice kid."

"Then it should work very well."

"Yes, I'm sure it will, John." Bernie opened the door. "I'll keep you informed."

Bernie closed the door and started for his car. "Smoke, I wonder if John knows what he's doing. The last I heard from David Suiter's mother, he was doing undercover work with the Metropolis Police Department."

*   *   *

Bernie returned home leaving his car in the driveway for afternoon calls. Letting himself in the front door, he stopped by the table in the foyer and picked up the mail that Charlotte had sorted for him.

"Meow?"

"Don't think there's anything for you today, Smoke," said Bernie. Several days ago, he'd received a sample package of kitty treats from the local pet store. Since then Smoke started watching the mail with Bernie.

Taking the small stack of envelopes to his study, Bernie sat at his desk. Smoke curled up on a chair until Charlotte knocked on the door then opened it.

"Yes?"

"Lunch is ready, Father, and a David Suiter called. He said he would be here in time for lunch tomorrow if that's all right." She gave Bernie a quizzical look.

"Thank you, Charlotte. I'll be right there. And David Suiter is a young priest in training. Bishop Murray told me this morning that he will be assigned as a student priest to St. Mark's for an indefinite time – at least for the summer."

"He will be living here?"

"Yes. I hope that's no problem. He's single and should be no trouble. Supposed to help me since I'm under so much stress I can't tell the difference between an accident and a murder." Bernie couldn't keep the sarcasm from his voice and the frown from his brow.

Charlotte frowned. "Father, I got no problem with cleaning up after another priest, or cooking extra – especially if he likes meat – but I think *they* are pressuring the bishop to get rid of you and I won't stand for that." Charlotte stood as tall as her five feet one inch would allow her to. Hands on her hips, she dared anyone to go against her desires.

Bernie laughed. "I think you might be right Charlotte. I told the bishop he could move me out and take my church, but I won't leave this town until Miriam's murderer is found."

"They're a bunch of idiots down at the police station – all except my nephew."

"Well, maybe having another priest around will give me time to snoop a little and find what Hollohan can't seem to find."

"Or *won't* find. I certainly hope so, Father and if I can ever help in any way, you just say the word."

"I appreciate that. Now, let's see what good things you fixed for lunch."

"Cream of broccoli soup and apple cobbler." She smiled at Smoke who leaped to Bernie's shoulder. "And for you, I have some shredded tuna."

"Meow."

"I think that means, 'Thank you,'" said Bernie. "And the soup sounds wonderful. Tomorrow you might want to fix something with meat for David. I knew him as a young boy. He used to be a big eater and I doubt that he's changed a great deal."

Sixteen

Snoop left the church a little early so he would be there when David arrived. He strolled down the street with Smoke draped across his shoulders, enjoying the warm June morning. Last night's summer storm had cooled the mugginess from the air – at least for a few hours. By afternoon, the temperature would again be in the high 80's.

Whistling as he walked up the driveway, Bernie pulled the key from his pocket. He reached the door and Smoke made a little guttural noise and raised his head. "What's up, Smoke?" *He never growls like that except when he doesn't like someone. He hasn't met David yet.* "Do we have a visitor? Probably David. You'll like him, he's a nice kid – or at least he used to be."

He opened the door. Smoke leaped to the floor, ran to the study door and stood with his back arched, fur on end. Charlotte came from the kitchen and nodded her approval. "That cat knows what's what. You have a visitor. I put him in the study with a cup of coffee, like you said I should do."

"Aha, said Bernie. "Hollohan. I didn't see his

car. Not like him to be walking."

"I saw a cruiser drive away when I answered the door."

"Maybe he expects me to drive him back to the station – after he arrests me for something."

"He had a search warrant."

"For what?"

"He wouldn't say, but he looked around before he went in to wait for you."

Bernie smiled at the sour look on Charlotte's face and Smoke's bushy fur. Neither cared much for the sergeant. Bernie was frustrated with the man, but he knew the sergeant was only doing his job.

"Thank you, Charlotte. If our student priest should arrive, let me know immediately."

"Yes sir, Father Bernie." She started to the kitchen muttering to herself, but Bernie heard her parting words, "…wish that man would just leave us alone."

He smiled again and reached for the study door. Smoke leaped into the room ahead of him and stood, back arched, between his master and the man who always seemed to bring trouble. Detective Hollohan rose as Bernie entered.

"Please stay seated," said Bernie. "Smoke, it's all right. Come and sit with me." Bernie sat in the winged back chair across from Hollohan and the gray cat leaped to his lap.

"What are they accusing me of this time?" Bernie didn't wait for Hollohan to speak.

"What makes you think you're accused of anything? Feeling guilty?"

Bernie shook his head. "If you had news of my wife's murderer, you would've said so. Since that's not the case, you must be searching for a reason to haul me in and charge me."

"You have to admit, you're still my most likely suspect," said Hollohan. "I have a search warrant. I need to look through your house."

"Mind telling me what you are looking for? Maybe I can save you the trouble and tell you where to look."

Hollohan watched Bernie's expression. "A missing chalice from the church – very expensive – with gems embedded around the side. The caller said you had it the day before it disappeared."

"You know, Sergeant, if this wasn't such a serious case, I could almost laugh at these childish antics. Of course, you'll find the chalice in my house. The person who killed my wife had a key to my door – and apparently still has it. You won't find it where my housekeeper would see it, because she would recognize it and tell me immediately. My guess is you'll find it in my bedroom closet, far corner of the top shelf. No fingerprints, of course – except mine from serving the Eucharist Sunday."

"Snoop, you are either guilty or very astute. I'm almost able to believe you if I just had another suspect. You were only here two days. No one knew you or your wife. Unless someone broke in – which we know didn't happen – then it had to be someone who knew her. And no one did. You can't even give me the names of former boyfriends."

"Sergeant, I told you before and I will continue to tell you until the world comes to an end, I loved my wife more than my own life. I will never forgive myself for not staying home with her that night. I will never again let a common meeting of the church or any other organization take precedence over important matters of life. Miriam and I never talked about former friends. It wasn't important. In the ten years we had together, we had no reason to reach outside our marriage for close friendships."

Smoke raised his head and twitched his ear toward the door. "Excuse me," said Snoop, "I think my housekeeper wants me."

Hollohan's eyes widened as the tap at the door followed the cat's warning. Bernie opened the door. Before he stepped outside to talk to Charlotte, he saw Smoke positioned himself just inside the door so that if Hollohan tried to leave the room he would have to step on him. He smiled as he closed the study door.

"You have a visitor, Father. The young priest."

"Thank you Charlotte." Bernie walked quickly to the front door where David waited inside the foyer. Charlotte returned to the kitchen.

"Sorry to keep you waiting, David," said Bernie. "How are you? Good to see you again."

"I wasn't sure you would remember me."

"Of course I remember you. How could I forget the kid who followed me around until you got in junior high and found other activities?"

David smiled and shook Father Snoop's hand.

"David, I had hoped to have some time to talk when you got here, but I need to ask you a question which might seem blunt, but necessary. Is Hollohan aware that we know each other?"

"Hollohan?" Except for the slight rise of color, David's face showed no understanding of the question, or the man's name.

Ignoring David's feigned ignorance, Bernie continued. "A further question – is he supposed to know you if he meets you here?"

"Father…"

"We don't have time to backpedal and set our stories."

"He's here?"

Bernie nodded and David's face paled. "All right," said Bernie, "you just answered both questions. Let me handle this and we'll talk later." He led the young man to the study.

"Sorry about the interruption, Sergeant. David, this is Sergeant Hugh Hollohan with the Metropolis Police Department. Sergeant, meet my new student intern, David Suiter, who is doing his practicum with St. Mark's for the rest of the summer. David, Sergeant Hollohan is investigating my wife's murder as well as a number of strange happenings at St. Mark's – all since I moved here, I might add, which puts me as number one suspect for anything that happens."

Sergeant Hollohan stretched his hand to greet David. "I'm glad to meet you young man. Don't let any of Snoop's brushes with the law rub off on you while you're here. Maybe you can even keep him out of trouble."

"Well, I'll certainly try," said David. He smiled at Bernie then turned back to Hollohan. "The only law they taught me in seminary was the Law of Moses, but if I'm going to live in the city, I suppose I need to learn about the other kind as well."

Smoke had been sitting on the chair arm swinging his head from speaker to speaker. Bernie hadn't introduced him, so Smoke gave a very loud "Meow" and tapped Snoop's arm. Bernie chuckled and picked the cat up. "Sorry about that, my friend. David, this is Holy Smoke. Smoke, meet David. He'll be living here for the next few months."

Surprised, David reached his hand to the cat. He let Smoke smell him first then stroked the top of Smoke's head. "I'm glad to meet you Smoke. I'm sure we'll become pals as long as I don't tread on your tail, your territory or your master."

Smoke leaned forward, licked David's fingers and purred his approval of this new addition to the household.

"I'm sure Father Snoop will help you learn the ways of the law," said Hollohan as Charlotte tapped on the door and opened it far enough to say, "Lunch is served, Father."

"Will you join us, Sergeant?"

"Thanks, but I have what I came after." Bernie lifted his eyebrows and Hollohan actually smiled. "I already looked and it was right where you said it would be."

"Which means either I put it there, or know the criminal mind well enough to know that the best place to hide something you want found is in a logical place."

"Snoop, I hope you are simply a natural at snooping and not a criminal. Good luck to you, young man."

Snoop walked with Hollohan to the door while Charlotte took David upstairs to his room where he could freshen up before lunch. Smoke stood beside Bernie until the sergeant had gone out the door, then he ran for the kitchen where Charlotte would give him his lunch treat. Bernie watched Hollohan walk down the drive to the sidewalk, wondering how he was going to carry that chalice back to the station on foot. A split second later the cruiser rounded the corner, stopped and picked him up. Bernie smiled. *Tried to catch me unaware.*

He met David in the dining room and they sat at one end of the long table as Charlotte set bowls of steaming fresh vegetable soup before them, the aroma of homemade flavor filling the room. Both men breathed deeply.

"Smells wonderful," said David.

"It will taste as good as it smells," Bernie said as Charlotte left the room for the rest of their lunch. Bernie leaned toward David and whispered, "She loves flattery." He winked as the door flew open and Charlotte returned with the sandwiches.

"I do not," she said.

"Don't let him get to you, Charlotte. Anything that smells this good has to be good – and everyone likes a compliment now and again. Right, Bernie?"

"Are you fishing for one?"

They both laughed and Charlotte set a plate of sandwiches between them – chicken salad and pimento cheese. She left and returned with a bowl of fruit for dessert.

"If you don't mind, Father Bernie," she said, "I need to run to the store and lay in some supplies for the weekend. Baker's is having a meat sale. I'm sure Father David eats meat – unless you would rather I didn't cook it at all." Charlotte stood lips pursed waiting for the *right* answer.

"That will be fine, Charlotte. David is a growing boy and needs all his protein. You might check for some eggplant and squash while you're at it."

Charlotte left and David looked at Snoop. "I'd forgotten you're a vegetarian," he said. "I can get along without meat if it bothers you."

"It's not against my religion, David. It's just a matter of taste. I never learned to eat meat when I was a child so I don't care for it now. I eat occasional fish and dairy products. Charlotte is the one who has a problem with it. She thinks it's sinful not to like steak or fried chicken. I'm sure Holy Smoke will appreciate having more of it around. He's a growing cat."

"How old is he?"

"I found him in early April during the fire at the church. The vet said he was about six to eight months old then."

"That's why you named him Holy Smoke?"

Snoop smiled and nodded. He was glad to have someone to talk to while he ate. It was even nicer to have someone to smile with.

Seventeen

"It's such a beautiful day," said Bernie, as he and David finished lunch. "We can walk over to the church and I'll show you around and explain the layout."

"That sounds like a plan to me. I have a car, but was hoping we lived close enough to walk. I need the exercise as well to save money on gas."

"Not much different than when I went to school," said Snoop. "Never enough money to cover all the necessities, much less a few luxuries."

David and Bernie started out the door and Smoke leaped to Bernie's shoulder before he could close the door. David laughed. "Does he go with you often?"

"Only when he wants to – which is most of the time."

"Folks don't mind a cat in the church?"

Bernie laughed. "They did until he walked out of the kitchen with a mouse in his mouth in the middle of the women's meeting."

David laughed with Bernie and Smoke said, "Meow."

"He didn't eat it, but took it to the custodian who was there that day. He made it very clear he expected Les to dispose of it properly. Since then, no one says anything. There are still some who frown when they see him, but mostly he sleeps on a pillow on a bookshelf in my office."

They walked for a few minutes in silence then David asked, "Do you mind talking about it?"

Bernie knew he meant the murder. "No, actually, you already know Hollohan's view. I would like for you to hear my side."

As they strolled to the church, Bernie told David his side of the story – Miriam's murder, thefts at the church, the fire that left a lot of smoke damage. He told him of his suspicions, that someone from the church killed his wife and Father Jones, but he had no idea of a motive. He knew David already had all the facts as recorded by Hollohan.

David gave Bernie a look of awe – much as he used to do when he was a young boy entering junior high school. "How did you know I'm working for Hollohan? Even the bishop doesn't know."

Bernie laughed. "All you ever talked about when you were a boy was being a cop. Your dream was to be undercover. Besides..." His eyes twinkled. "...I hear from your proud mama every once in a while."

It was David's turn to laugh. "I'm glad you know. I hated the thoughts of keeping secrets from you. We made a good team when I was in school. Remember when someone broke into the school and got in some lockers?"

"Yes, the police accused the Petre boy because someone saw him near the school that day."

"But you and I proved he was innocent and found the real culprit."

Bernie smiled. "That seems so long ago, but we did work well together. Maybe we can do it again. I feel like I've made progress, but I keep missing something."

"Maybe you're too close to the situation. You need to bounce your theories around with someone."

"I think you're right. Maybe you and I can list our theories and see where they connect and come up with a solution."

"I hope so, Father. I hope so. I've read all of Hollohan reports. I didn't find anything about former boyfriends."

"Hollohan asked, but he didn't stop with *former*. He still thinks either I killed Miriam or she had a lover on the side who became angry with her."

"Either one is utterly ridiculous," said David. "I didn't know Miriam – met her at your wedding –

but anyone who knows you would know that was impossible. You would no more hurt her than you would cut off your right arm. And I would bet my bottom dollar that she never had eyes for anyone but you – at least after you were married. How about before you were married? She must have had boyfriends."

"Hollohan asked me that too. He thought it was rather strange that I didn't know. Miriam was wearing a diamond on her left hand the first day I met her. We were both immediately drawn to each other, but she was a student – much younger than I. The next time I saw her, the ring was missing. She was left-handed, so I couldn't help but notice. Afraid she may have lost it, I had to comment. She laughed, said she'd made a mistake and gave it back to the young man. She never told me his name; I never asked. We never talked about former friends. It didn't matter."

"It might matter now. If he somehow caught up with her and…"

"She did receive gifts – even after we were married –candy and flowers. She threw them away. Letters she burned without opening them. I never questioned her – never saw where or who they were from."

"Even if the murderer were an old boyfriend, how would he get in the house? Had to be someone with a key, or she opened the door because she knew him."

"But, she didn't know anyone here. She had the flu when we moved in on Saturday. Sunday morning she was still ill so didn't go to church to meet any of the church people. She was killed on Monday."

"Is it possible someone in the congregation might have known her before? They probably wouldn't tell you and she didn't know about it."

"Anything is possible, I suppose. Maybe someone from college?"

"Did she have any college yearbooks? Journals she kept? Pictures from her school days? Friends she kept in touch with?"

"David, you're making my head spin. I should have thought of all those things."

"No you shouldn't have, because this is too close to you. If you were looking at another family from a distance, you would see everything differently."

"She kept a journal all the time. Each year, on our anniversary, she began a new one and placed the old one in her cedar chest. I haven't looked. They were personal and I promised her I would never look in them – even if she died. I told her I would burn them without reading them."

"Is that what she wanted you to do? And did you?"

"We were joking with each other. She said she really didn't care if I read them. I told her I would listen if she wanted to read them to me, but I would never touch her journals." She laughed and called me silly, but I felt very strongly that something that personal should be kept sacred. But, to answer your question, no, I didn't burn them – yet. I hadn't even thought about them. They must still be in her cedar chest, which I've not been able to make myself open yet."

"We'll have to do it, Father. I'll do the looking if you don't want to – if only to find some names of friends that we can contact. Someone who might know whom she dated and who might still hold a grudge all these years. We can always check the school library for archived copies of the yearbooks."

"I know you're right, David and I'll get the journals for you tonight. I don't mind you doing it, but I'm glad Hollohan didn't ask for them. Here's the church. I'll show you around and introduce you to Alice, our secretary."

"It's a beautiful old church," said David. "They just don't make them like this anymore."

"We're still in the process of renovating from the fire. Our congregation will meet in our own sanctuary this Sunday for the first time in two and a half months."

"You held services somewhere else?"

"Yes, in the Baptist Church across the street."

They walked up the stone steps and into the narthex. David stopped to look into the sanctuary. "Truly beautiful," he said.

"Our offices are down the corridor to the right at the end of the narthex," said Bernie. "Alice's office is the first door and the choir room is next. The board room and then the pastor's office is at the end of the hall. We'll take a quick tour and come back to the offices."

Bernie and David went to basement with its fellowship hall, kitchen and furnace room then back to the first floor Sanctuary and offices. The trustees had outfitted a corner of Bernie's office for David with a desk, file cabinets, computer complete with monitor, printer, scanner and internet service. Bernie had to smile at how quickly they worked to get setup for a student assistant when he'd had to almost beg for what he needed.

They stepped into the secretary's office just as Alice folded the last bulletin for Sunday. "Alice," said Father Snoop, "this is David Suiter, our student priest for the rest of the summer – and beyond if it works out for him. David this is Alice Sterns. If you have any question about the church, or anyone in it, Alice can supply the answer. And I might add that I've found if you expect her to keep a confidence, she won't breathe a word even if she is tempted by ladies bearing chocolate cake with thick creamy icing."

Alice turned pink and laughed. "Thank you for the compliment, Father. I was raised in a Christian home. My daddy always said, 'Girl if you make a promise, you better keep it or you'll regret it the rest of your life. If someone tells you a secret, it stops with you. Glad to meet you… eh… what do I call a student priest? Father? Reverend? Daddy?"

Snoop and David laughed with her and David said, "David is fine. Until I earn that seminary degree, I don't feel I have the right to be called by any title."

"I'll introduce him in church as Reverend David. That should satisfy the sticklers for titles, but David is a good name. We'll use it."

"Well, I'm glad to meet you David. Anything I can help you with?"

"As a matter of fact, there might be," he said. "Do you have a pictorial directory of the membership? It would help me get to know the folks quicker."

"We sure do. Actually, it's only a year old, so it's almost up to date. It was out of date by the time it went to press. Do you have one of these Father Bernie?"

"Yes, I do, thank you. And it is helpful. I'll get mine and take it home with us. We can go over them together tonight. I'll fill David in on any of the changes you gave me."

"If you have any questions, you know you can call me at home any time before ten o'clock. My husband gets up at four to go to work – so he doesn't like calls after that – except for emergencies, of course."

"Thanks, Alice," said David. "We probably won't need to do that, but it's good to know we can if necessary."

Eighteen

The rest of the afternoon David and Bernie spent going over files of people who would be important for David to know – Senior Warden, Personnel chair, organist, Choir Director, Junior Warden other leaders of the congregation.

The intercom buzzed and Bernie looked up surprised. He'd told Alice not to disturb them so... he pressed the button. "Yes?"

"Sorry to bother you Father. I'm leaving. Do you want me to lock up?"

"Is it five o'clock already?"

Alice laughed. "Yes, it is."

"I heard the phone a few times. Anything important."

"Not really, except Charlotte. She said she'd talk to you when you got home."

"Thanks Alice. Yes, please lock up. We'll go out the alley door."

Smoke stood on the shelf where he had been sleeping, stretched then jumped to Bernie's desk.

"Is it supper time Smoke?"

"Meow."

"Charlotte always bugs me about keeping regular meals. She says Smoke has a better sense of hunger time than I do. I suspect that's why she called – to remind me you're a growing boy and need your dinner."

David laughed. "I'm hardly a boy anymore, but if it makes her happy to think so, I won't complain."

"We do have a lot to do when we get home. Today is Wednesday and Charlotte leaves early for a class she's taking at the University. But she'll have something good waiting for us."

"Then what are we waiting for? Right Smoke?"

"Meow!" Smoke leaped to Bernie's shoulders. They went out the alley door and down to 32nd Street and home.

Bernie was right. Charlotte left a pot of beef stew and a pan of cornbread. A note was propped against the soup tureen that held the stew. "Sorry about the beef, Father. You can pick it out. Give it to Smoke. He knows what's good."

David and Bernie had a good laugh while Smoke sat patiently waiting for Bernie to dish up his dinner. Bernie and David sat in the kitchen to eat rather than carry everything to the dining room and back.

When they finished David cleared the table and Bernie went directly to Miriam's cedar chest in his bedroom. Smoke jumped from his shoulder onto the bed and then to the top of the chest. David followed him to the door.

"Smoke, you'll have to move or you'll fall off when I open the lid. Come on in, David. Maybe you can hold Smoke while I open the chest."

Bernie pushed in the lock. It clicked and the lid lifted easily. He sat for a minute staring, blinking rapidly to cut off the rush of emotion. David understood and waited holding Smoke who squirmed to get down.

"Sorry," said Snoop. "This is more difficult than I thought it would be. I should have done it long ago while I was still too numb to feel anything."

"Things like this take time," said David. "You can only do it when you're ready."

"Are you sure you aren't really going to become a Priest?" Snoop looked up at the young man and smiled.

"That's not on my agenda."

"God has a way of changing agendas."

David laughed and set Smoke on the bed. Smoke immediately jumped into the chest and began rooting around. Snoop lifted a stack of journals from the chest. "These begin on our wedding day. The last one she placed there the day before she died. She would have begun a new one that evening.

Smoke pranced around on the plastic that

covered a large box. Bernie lifted it out. Bold black permanent marker spelled out the words: Wedding Dress. Under the box was another stack of journals. They began ten years before their wedding.

"She said she began writing in journals when she was twelve. The first had been a gift from her Aunt Dorothy – a writer, who was killed in a car accident when Miriam was only fifteen."

"These should cover any of her dating years. Do you want me to take them to my room and go through them, or would you rather do it?"

"Why don't we take them down to the study and work on them together? We'll put these back." He lifted the married years and started to put them back. "On the other hand, we don't know that someone didn't cause her some trouble that I don't know about. She wouldn't have complained. We'll take them just in case."

David heaved a sigh. "That's good thinking, Bernie – tough but right. I won't need to look at the later ones unless these reveal nothing."

"Come on Smoke, get out of there before I close the lid on you."

"Meow?" The cat let his front paws swipe over a stack of pictures, exposing the corner of another book of some kind. "What you got there, Smoke? Something we need to look at?"

Bernie moved the pictures aside and lifted the

books – two yearbooks, one from high school and one from college.

"Looks like we hit pay dirt," said David. "At least we can contact the school and learn more about any of these people."

"Good work, Smoke. Let's go look for clues."

Bernie closed the chest. Laden with journals and yearbooks, he and David went to the study. They sat at opposite sides of the large walnut desk and leafed through the books. A tap at the door brought their head up.

"Who would be in the house? Charlotte left before we got home."

Bernie walked to the door, opened it and stepped to the hallway. David followed with his hand on the gun in the back of his waistband.

"I'm sorry to bother you Father Bernie," said Charlotte. "I went to do some errands and pick up a few grocery items that were on sale before I go to my class tonight. I wanted you to know about the man that came this afternoon."

"What man? Is that what you called the church about?"

"Yes. Alice said you were busy, but she would see if you could talk. I told her I'd see you tonight. I would handle the problem."

"And did you? Handle the problem that is." Bernie smiled at her knowing there weren't many problems Charlotte couldn't handle.

"Yes, the man said you sent him to pick up your wife's cedar chest for a special auction for the children's fund. I told him you didn't leave any instructions for me. He showed me a paper that had your signature on it, but it didn't look like your writing. I told him he would have to come back when you were here because I didn't know anything about it. He said he was in a hurry and I should just tell him which room it was in and he would take care of everything. I'm sorry, Father, I lied to the man. I told him it was in your bedroom and you always locked the door and took the key with you."

At the mention of the cedar chest, David started laughing and Bernie joined. Charlotte looked confused, then angry.

Bernie laid a hand on her arm and said, "Charlotte, what you did was absolutely brilliant. You were very watchful. You were right. I didn't send anyone after that chest. In fact, David and I are looking through some keepsakes from it right now. If he had taken it, we wouldn't be able to do that. Do you know what he looked like? Where he was from? License number?"

Charlotte's face glowed with pleasure. "Did I really help you? Will it help catch that killer?"

"Anything you remember will certainly help, Charlotte."

"Just a minute." Charlotte left them standing by the study door looking quizzically at each other. She returned with a drawing tablet in her hand. "I've been taking art courses at the university. You told me I should follow my dream and I always wanted to be a police artist."

Bernie and David gave each other a surprised look. Charlotte opened her tablet and flipped through several pages of portraits in pencil and charcoal. From what the men could see, the drawings were very good.

"Here it is," she said. "I've still got some learning to do, but it looks pretty close to the man who came here this afternoon. I hope you don't mind me taking time out of my work to draw it."

Bernie took the tablet. David looked over his shoulder. They both opened their mouth, but nothing came out. Finally, Bernie said, "Charlotte this is wonderful. Why are you wasting your time cleaning house and cooking for a poor preacher?"

"Because I like to clean house and cook and you always appreciate my efforts. Is it really good?"

"It is. We'll get this to Detective Hollohan immediately. We'll tell him what you told us. He'll probably want to hear it from you. Can he call you at home later?"

"After ten o'clock. I'm on my way to my art class."

"What are these numbers at the corner of the

page?" David pointed to a combination of number and letters.

"Those are the numbers on the license plate of the truck. He backed into the drive so I could see them clearly from the window."

Again David and Bernie laughed. Smoke wrapped around Charlotte's ankles and purred as if giving her his compliments for a job well done.

"Charlotte, you go to your art class and enjoy. We'll just take this picture out and you can take the rest with you. Someone thinks there is something in that chest that is worth stealing. David and I will find out what it is. Thank you again for your help and awareness."

Nineteen

Charlotte left for her class and Bernie called Hollohan, who came immediately. "What's on your mind, Snoop? Ready to confess?"

"Sorry, Hollohan, but we had a strange occurrence this afternoon and thought you might be interested." Bernie told him what Charlotte had told them and showed him the picture and the license number.

"Why would anyone want your wife's cedar chest?"

"Apparently he remembered she kept the journals. He must have known about the cedar chest her aunt had given her and guessed she kept her journals in it. He figured he would be mentioned somewhere in those journals."

"I hope you're right, Snoop. So, where are the journals? Do you have them? And why didn't you mention them before?"

"Yes, I have them, thanks to Charlotte's quick thinking. I didn't mention them before because I was too caught up in my grief to even think about the journals. When I did remember, I didn't want the memories they would dredge up. David and I were just going through them and..."

"David? Your associate?"

"Yes, and your undercover cop."

Hollohan's eyebrows lifted as he glanced from Bernie to David and back to Bernie.

"He didn't tell me. I knew from the day Bishop Murray told me who was coming here. I've known David since he was in grade school and I correspond with his mother on occasion."

"How many others know?" Hollohan gave him a sour look.

"No one – unless Charlotte has guessed. She's not easily fooled."

"I see. Well, since the cat's out of the bag, so to speak..."

"Meow?" Smoke, ears laid back, tail thumping, glared at Hollohan with crossed eyes.

Bernie and David laughed. Holloway sputtered. "Not you," he said to Smoke. "Since we're all on the same page, mind if I help you look?"

"Why don't I get us some coffee," said Bernie.

The three of them went through the journals, finding nothing except one reference to becoming engaged to C.J. then meeting Bernie and breaking her engagement. C.J. was angry and promised to get even, but that had been twelve years ago. Surely, he'd found someone else and forgotten all about Miriam.

It was getting late. They hadn't forgotten the yearbooks; they were simply overlooked with so many journals. Bernie noticed them as he went to lock up after Hollohan left. David took several journals to bed with him. Tired as he was, Bernie wasn't ready for sleep. He flipped through the high school book, laid it aside and picked up the college yearbook. He began looking for men with the initials, C. J. Suddenly, he felt as if ice water had replaced his blood. He shivered. *That has to be the one, but how could he have murdered Miriam? He wasn't around, or was he? Should I call Hollohan? David? No, I'll check it out tomorrow then talk to David.*

It was almost dawn before exhaustion finally overtook him and Bernie slept until Smoke tapped his cheek, reminding him it was time for breakfast.

Charlotte met Snoop as he descended the stairs. "Good morning, Father," she said. "David is already at breakfast. He's been up and out for a three mile run. He doesn't lie abed like *some* people do."

Snoop smiled at Charlotte. In the short time he'd been at St. Mark's, he learned that Charlotte was a fussy, mother-hen type. He assumed she was more so since his wife's death.

Miriam would not have put up with it. "Thank you, Charlotte." He didn't add that David probably had more sleep than he had. She would have pressured him more.

"Good morning, David," Snoop said as he entered the dining room. "I'll join you as soon as I take care of Smoke."

"Charlotte said I should start without you. Hope you don't mind."

"Not at all. Sometimes I don't even bother with breakfast. A little coffee is all I need."

He went to the kitchen, fed Smoke and returned to the table, where he filled his cup with steaming hot coffee. "I took the yearbooks to bed with me last night. I think I've discovered something. I need to drive out to Oak Grove College and talk to some folks there."

"About the murder?"

"That and about a memorial gift I want to give to the college in Miriam's name. I haven't seen my friend Doctor Myers since the funeral in January. Like I said, Miriam and I never talked about the past, but I think Doctor Myers can fill me in."

"Shall I go with you?"

"No, I think you should go to the church – be visible – make some phone calls. It might be a good idea to check out some reservations – airports and motels and conferences."

"Recent or future?"

Snoop grinned. "I think you know the answer to

that," he said handing him a list. "Call me on my cell if you find out anything. If I learn anything from Doctor Myers, I'll call you."

"You be careful, Bernie. Don't go getting yourself in a jam."

"Now, what kind of trouble could I get into talking to the current president of the college and the retired president, who happens to be a friend? By the way, the college yearbook is on the study desk. You might want to browse through it. I've marked page 35."

Bernie finished his coffee and rose to go as Charlotte came in with food for him. "Father Bernie, you are not leaving this house before you get some protein in you. Sit down and eat these eggs."

Charlotte set the bowl of scrambled eggs before him. She even spooned some onto his plate, then placed her hands on her hips and dared him to refuse to eat. Bernie grinned at David, shrugged, and sat back in his chair. He finished half the eggs and while Charlotte went for more coffee, he made his escape.

"Tell her I won't be back for lunch," he said to David and left. David's laughter followed him into the foyer. Smoke ran after him and made a flying leap to Bernie's shoulder.

"Okay, Smoke," he said. "Let's go for a ride."

"Meow," answered his faithful companion.

Bernie's other faithful friend – his '69 VW Beetle – waited patiently in the garage for him. Bernie loved his car. One of the few arguments he and Miriam ever had was over him not getting rid of it. He would have given her anything her heart desired, but he would not give up his beloved car.

He folded his tall frame into the seat, Smoke settled beside him on the passenger seat. Bernie backed down the driveway and was soon cruising along on the expressway. "Smoke, I hope I'm wrong about my deductions, and yet, I feel deep in my bones that I'm right. If so, we can soon put this all behind us. Either way, I need to get this memorial settled."

Smoke stood on the seat with his front paws against the window so he could watch the passing traffic. Once out of the city, trees and houses began to replace tall buildings and people on sidewalks. Blue sky, dotted with white fluffy clouds, became more visible. The farther he drove, the more open the land – pastures with cattle and sheep grazing, wheat fields waving their golden heads, corn already two feet high.

Bernie sighed contentedly. "You would love it out here, Smoke. I do. I never was a city dweller. I like the wide-open spaces. Maybe someday…" Bernie let his rambling drift while he and Smoke enjoyed the scenery.

Twenty

While Snoop made his way out of town, David finished the bowl of scrambled eggs and rose to leave. "Good breakfast, Charlotte," he said when she came back into the room. "Oh, by the way, Father Bernie said he wouldn't be back in time for lunch."

"Humph," said Charlotte. "I suppose he'll skip it again. That man just won't eat right."

"Actually, I think he said something about having lunch with an old friend in Oak Grove." David crossed his fingers under the table as he fudged on the truth.

"Well, then, I'll fix you something nice," she said, meaning something non-vegetarian.

"Thank you," said David. "I'll just get a few papers from the study then walk to the church. Father had some tasks for me to do there. I'll call if I'm going to be late."

"I'm glad you're here, David," said Charlotte. "Father Bernie needs help – and not just in the church." She didn't give David a chance to respond, but took the dishes to the kitchen. David smiled. He agreed with Bernie. That woman was one sharp lady and knew far more than she would ever tell. He picked up the college yearbook and the note pad with Bernie's list. He glanced over the list and dropped both into his brief case. It was a beautiful day for a walk to the church.

"Good morning, Alice," he called as he passed the secretary's office. "Father Bernie won't be in this morning and I have some important calls to make. I'd rather not be disturbed unless it's an emergency."

"Lock your door. I'll field any calls or visitors."

"Thanks." David continued to the office he and Bernie shared. He pulled out the list and the yearbook. He glanced over the list and exhaled in a long slow whistle. What was Bernie thinking? Was it possible…?

He flattened the list on his desk, read it again and reached for the phone. Hollohan had to know about this. While he waited for Hollohan to answer, he opened the yearbook to the page Bernie had marked – senior pictures. One had a red circle around it.

"Hollohan." David almost dropped the phone.

"David here. I think we hit pay dirt. Bernie went to Oak Grove to check with the former president of the school about Miriam's former fiancé. He left a list of calls for me to make and a picture circled in the yearbook. I'm going to need some help with these calls and I think we can close this case very soon."

"Really? What you got. Read me the list."

"One – Check airlines. See if Charles Lewis was actually on flight 2937 to San Francisco on January 4. Two – Check with Radisson Hotel. See if he was actually registered and if he was physically there. Three – Check with Business Associations of the North West and see if he was registered at the conference and if he attended all the sessions. Four – check with rental car agencies at the airport. See if a car was rented on January 4 – possibly under another similar name, and I might add another," said David. "We might want to double check with his wife and see if she actually watched him get on the plane and watch the plane take off."

"Does he suspect his Senior Warden?"

"Sounds like it. The picture he circled – Charles James Lewis. Miriam's journals mentioned being engaged to C. J. and him not being too happy about the break-up."

"We checked all the items on that list," said Hollohan.

"We checked to see if he was registered. Did we check to see if he was actually there? Could someone else have sat in on the meetings for him? Was he on the plane when it took off and landed?"

"You're beginning to sound like Snoop," grumbled Hollohan. "But you're right. We'll go back and check the details. You want to check with the wife?"

"Sure, I'll give her a call – maybe ask her if he's in town and if he can stop by here on his way home from work today. I'm new. I need help in the administration end of the church."

"Sure you are," said Hollohan and left David with a buzzing phone in his hand. David laughed and reached for the directory. He looked up the Lewis' number, dialed and waited.

"Hello."

"Mrs. Lewis? This is David Suiter at the church."

"Yes, David, what can I do for you?"

"Is your husband home – or in town?"

"No to both," she said. "He went to Cincinnati this morning, but his plane is due in at four. Do you need something?"

"I just need to talk to him about some administration questions that I don't understand. I didn't want to bother Father Bernie. I'm sure you understand."

"Sure, poor man is still grieving." Patricia didn't sound like she really believed that. Like many of the church folks, she irrationally blamed Bernie for the loss of their beloved pastor, Father

Jones. "Sometimes Chuck calls before he leaves the airport. Shall I have him call you if he should call?"

"I would appreciate that. Tell him Father Bernie is out of town for the day and I need to finish a report for school."

"Where did Father go? To visit his wife's grave – again? He really should be getting over it by now."

David could almost see the sneer on her face. Apparently, that didn't apply to the folks at St. Mark's. He forced himself to remember his reason for calling and tried to ignore her insensitivity.

"Actually, he went to see the president of Oak Grove College about a memorial for Miriam at the school. She was the former president's secretary for the four years she was there." He paused then changed the subject before she could comment. "Will you be picking Chuck up at the airport? Maybe I could go for you and we could talk while I drive him home."

"Well...yes ...I, eh, always drop him off and pick him up. He, eh, hates to drive in the airport traffic." Patricia seemed to be hedging, then gained her control and finished, "I appreciate your offer, David, but we had planned to go to a movie and dinner from the airport."

"That's all right. I understand. My sister enjoys watching the planes take off and land. She likes to go, even if she isn't meeting anyone."

"Actually, I'm not a flyer myself and I don't care for planes. I always drop Chuck off at the door and pick him up there. He likes to fly and doesn't mind finding the plane by himself."

"Well, enjoy your dinner and movie and have him call me if you hear from him earlier. If not, I'll get the information from Father Bernie when he gets home later tonight – unless he spends the night with his friend, President Myers."

David was aware that he was maybe setting Bernie up and thought he ought to call him and warn him that Chuck might react. He would wait to see if he heard from him first. After all what could he do from Cincinnati?

David hung up the phone and sat drumming his fingers on the desk. Patricia did not see her husband board the plane the night Miriam was killed. She only had his word that he left. He could very well have rented a car and driven to the manse after Bernie left for the board meeting.

Twenty-one

While David and Hollohan followed up on calls, Bernie entered the college town of Oak Grove. Following the paved, curved road through the campus, he stopped in the parking lot beside Myers Hall, the new college administrative building named for the former president, Calvin Myers. Bernie sat for a minute or two, taking in the view – buildings, trees full of leaves, students strolling hand in hand. He let the memories wash over him and run off like a sudden shower. Then as if the sun parted gloomy clouds, he smiled at Holy Smoke and opened the car door.

"Come on Smoke. Want to walk a little before we go in?"

"Meow," said Smoke and tugged at the halter leash as he leaned on the window watching a gray squirrel near a huge oak tree. When Bernie opened the door, Smoke leaped over him and went to investigate the squirrel. Bernie closed the car and followed him.

Holy Smoke sat back on his haunches, looking surprised when the squirrel ran up the tree chattering at them. He watched while the squirrel continued to scold from the safety of his lofty limb. Bernie laughed and lifted Smoke to his shoulders.

"It's all right, Smoke. He was afraid you wanted him for lunch. Let's see if the president is in this morning."

Bernie walked into the waiting area of the president's office. The secretary, who seemed very young, looked up and smiled. "Good morning, sir – and kitty." She giggled like the schoolgirl that she was and stood to touch Smoke's soft fur. "Can I help you?"

Must be a freshman. Bernie smiled at her lack of correct grammar. "Good morning," he said. "I would like to speak with President Evans. Is he in?"

"Yes sir, he's in, but he asked not to be disturbed this morning. Did you have an appointment?"

"No, I just drove down from Metropolis because I had some free time and it was such a beautiful day. Why don't you buzz him and see if he will talk to me about a memorial gift to the college in memory of my wife, a former student?"

"I don't know if I should…" The girl chewed on the end of her pencil.

"That's all right," said Bernie. "I'll just walk in and you won't have to make the decision." He started toward the door.

"Wait a minute, sir. I'll...I'll ask him. What's your name?"

"Father Bernard Snoop and I want to talk to him about a gift in memory of Miriam Parker Snoop."

His extremely full calendar suddenly cleared and President Evans personally escorted Bernie into his office. Seated across from the president, Bernie listened attentively to the possibilities for memorial gifts – scholarship funds, building funds, endowment funds.

"What about something personal – like a fountain, or tree or set of research books?"

"That could be a possibility," said Dr. Evans. "As a pastor of a church, you understand some of the problems with that approach."

"Yes," said Bernie. "I've had gifts given to the church with so many strings attached that we had to turn down the gift."

"I'm glad you understand. Some people don't. Why don't you take these pamphlets, brochures and lists of dreams of the college with you? Take your time and decide what would be best for your situation. Then we'll meet again whenever you say."

"Thank you, Sir. I'll give you a call the next time. I'm sorry to come without calling first, but this was an unplanned trip and I thought I would take a chance on you being in your office."

Bernie rose and Smoke took his place on Bernie's shoulder. Dr. Evans shook Bernie's hand and walked him to the door. "I'll look forward to our next visit."

Loaded with information about possibilities and amounts for a memorial gift, Bernie opened the VW door. Smoke leaped to his seat and Bernie dropped his load of materials on the floor behind the driver's seat.

"Well, Smoke, looks like we have a lot of choices. As soon as we can put this murder business behind us, I'll be able to think more clearly. Now, let's go see my friend, Doctor Myers."

Rolling Hills, a sprawling suburban housing development, where the former president of the college, Doctor Calvin Myers lived was about twenty minutes away. Bernie and Miriam had visited the Myers many times during the time they lived in Oak Grove. Then they were only minutes away. Now it was an hour and a half from Metropolis.

Driving under the stone arch with the words Rolling Hills printed across the top – each letter embedded in its own stone – Bernie turned to his traveling companion. "What do you think, Smoke? Aren't these lovely homes – real yards with trees and flowers."

Smoke, front paws against the side window, meowed as if giving him a positive response.

"We turn right at the next four-way stop and drive a quarter of a mile. Homes on the hills look inviting. Not sure I'd want those driveways in the winter, though."

Smoke slapped his tail against the back of the seat in agreement.

"Well, here we are. There's Dr. Myers' house."

The house looked like an enlarged gingerbread house surrounded by trees, shrubs, flowers and a rock garden that cascaded down the slope to the sidewalk. "No mowing and no mud slides on that yard," said Bernie. He turned up the driveway that circled the house to the garage in back. Bernie stopped at the front of the house.

Bernie opened his door and stood beside the car. Smoke jumped to the ground and began to explore unusual scents and sights. Bernie walked up the two steps to the porch and rang the doorbell.

The door opened and Doctor Myers looked up at the tall, lanky man on his doorstep. A smile spread across his face. He pushed his glasses up on his nose and wrapped his arms around his friend.

"Bernie! What a pleasant surprise. What brings you to our little corner of the world? Come in, come in."

"Sorry I didn't call ahead, but it was a last minute decision to drive down here. I was over at the college to see about a memorial for Miriam."

Doctor Myers backed up to give room for Bernie to enter. Smoke slipped between their legs. "What was that? I hope it wasn't that blasted squirrel. He's been trying for weeks to get in the house."

Bernie chuckled. Smoke jumped to Bernie's shoulder so Bernie could introduce him to the man. "This is Holy Smoke. He has become my constant companion."

"Hello, Holy Smoke. I'm glad you're not a squirrel. You are welcome to explore the house and take care of any moving vermin you might happen to run upon."

Smoke blinked and jumped down to do just that – explore the house. Doctor Myers called to his wife. "Hannah, we'll have a guest for lunch and some coffee in the study now would be nice. Come, join us."

Hannah stepped into the foyer. "Bernie! How good to see you. I'll have fresh coffee in a few minutes."

"Good to see you, Hannah. That's a wonderful aroma of something coming from the kitchen, but don't go to any bother."

Hannah laughed at his not-so-subtle hint. "No, bother for an old friend," she said. "I just took some banana nut bread out of the oven."

"Oh, by the way, Hannah," said Doctor Myers, "if you see a gray, furry something creeping around corners, it's not that squirrel we've been fighting. It's only Father Snoop's cat, Holy Smoke."

Hannah laughed and returned to the kitchen. Bernie and Doctor Myers moved into the study. "I know you must still be grieving and missing your beautiful wife, Bernie. How can I help you? Have they caught the killer yet?"

Bernie shook his head. "I hope you can give me some information that will help. As strange as it may seem, Miriam and I never talked about our lives before we met. We lived every day so fully that we just didn't seem to have room for things that were in the past."

Myers laughed. "Miriam was my secretary for the four years she was in our school. That was her motto then, too. She always said, 'Yesterday is gone. We can either build on what we did, or forget it, but we can't hold on to it, so why waste today's precious minutes?' I thought that was pretty insightful for a young girl, but she believed it."

"And it was wonderful just living each day with her, but now I find I know nothing of her past – things which might help us solve her murder."

"Miriam was a hard worker, a very bright student with an outgoing personality, but I'm sure you knew all that. You're looking for something specific."

"Yes, her friends. She never mentioned them except for a couple of girls with whom she exchanged Christmas cards. I guess I'm looking for boyfriends who might not have let go emotionally."

"Ah. Don't be tempted to blame an old flame, Bernie. That's jealously, not good detecting."

"I couldn't agree more, except I read her journals yesterday because I remembered she was engaged when we met. The next time I saw her, she said the engagement was over. I didn't give it much thought then, but now I wonder how the young man reacted when she returned his ring."

Doctor Myers said nothing, but listened with his eyes and well as his ears. Bernie continued. "In her journals, she doesn't name persons, only gives initials. For the date she met me, she said, C.J. was very angry about her breaking the engagement and told her she would be sorry. She wrote, 'he'll get over it.' But, did he? Could a person carry a grudge for so long?"

"It's possible, Bernie, but not very probable. I remember that young man. I didn't particularly like him. He was cocky and arrogant – wanted to be called by his initials. He thought it set him apart – made him important."

"So C. J. was his name – at least the name he used? Was that his first and last initials?"

"No, first and middle. He was an insolent young

man. He often became angry if Miriam wasn't ready to go when he stopped by for her. He thought she should drop everything and jump the minute he came in – even if it wasn't time for her to leave. I could never understand what she saw in him in the first place. I told her she deserved better. She just laughed and said he would change."

"What kind of student was he? What was his major? His full name? Where did he come from?"

"Careful, Bernie, don't..." Doctor Myers took off his glasses and polished them. Bernie waited. "Charles was from a well to do family, not an especially good student. He got a degree in Business Administration. Probably wouldn't have except he wasn't above paying someone to do his homework, or even stealing a test for him. I lost track of him after they graduated and Miriam married you."

"Was he from this area?"

"No, he was from Metropolis – the east side, I think."

Bernie felt his heart thumping, but kept his voice calm. "Do you remember his full name?"

"How could I forget? I had enough confrontations with him, both over his grades and over Miriam. Once I even had to call in his father and warn him if Charles – I refused to call him C. J. – didn't straighten up, we would have to expel him. That only brought out the checkbook with an offer of a million dollars to overlook his faults – which, of course, I refused."

"Charles?"

"Charles James Lewis – C.J. for short."

"Did he ever go by Chuck?"

"His father called him that. Do you know him?"

"I'm afraid I do. Excuse me, Doctor Myers; I need to make a call. I'll use my cell."

Bernie lifted his cell phone to punch in the numbers, but it began chirping before he hit the first number. Surprised, he dropped it, but recovered his grip before the phone hit to the floor. "David?"

"Yes."

"I was just going to call you." Calvin rose to leave, but Bernie motioned for him to stay. "I was on the right track. What did you find?"

"You sure were on the right track. Hollohan and I are on the way to Oak Grove. Checked all your list. His wife said he went to Cincinnati this morning. She never watches him board a plane or waits for the plane to take off. Checked with the rental cars at the airport. He rented one under the name C.J. Louis, spelled L-O-U-I-S, not L-E-W-I-S. Not the first or the last time he rented from them. He rented one today. Checked flights to Cincinnati. Not on any of them. He called me a few minutes after I talked to Patricia who said she'd called him.

I had a fictitious question about the church. Anyway, he knows where you are and my guess is he'll show up there on some pretext."

"Not likely. He's no dummy. He'll know we're on to him. We'll keep an eye out for him though."

"Be careful. We've alerted the Oak Grove Police. Call them if you suspect anything unusual."

Before Bernie could answer, a shot rang out shattering the front window of the study. "You mean like that? Someone just took a shot at the house. Got to go."

Hannah screamed and ran into the study, Smoke right behind her. Smoke leaped to Bernie's shoulder and Hannah stood in the doorway wringing her hands.

"Hannah, get down," Doctor Myers yelled as he dropped to the floor. Bernie, who still had his cell in his hand, called nine-one-one.

Another shot sent a vase on the bookshelf shattering to the floor.

Twenty-two

"I hear sirens," said Calvin. "I know our police force is on the ball, but that is really a quick response."

"That was my assistant on the cell. He called Oak Grove Police. He and Sergeant Hollohan from Metropolis are on their way. I'll explain in a little bit."

Outside a lot of shouting, sirens and squealing of tires filled the air. Bernie crept to the window and chanced a look out to the street. "Looks like three police cruisers, Hollohan's Ford, and an unknown vehicle – probably a rental."

The doorbell rang, followed by pounding. "Father Bernie," the visitor called. "Are you all right?"

"It's David," said Bernie. "I'll get it. You stay down, Mrs. Myers just in case it's not him."

Smoke looked from Bernie to Hannah and ran to her side. She reached for him and held him tighter than he was used to anyone holding him, but he didn't complain. Bernie and Doctor Myers could see David standing on the stoop examining the shattered glass beside the door.

"Is anyone hurt?" David looked up as the door opened.

"No, we're fine. Just scared Smoke and Mrs. Myers. Did you get him?"

"Yeah, we got him. Good afternoon Doctor Myers."

"You remember David Suiter, don't you?" Bernie turned to his friend. "He was a student here."

"Yes, I do remember. You were from Bernie's former church when he came to Oak Grove. You studied law, I believe."

"You have a good memory, sir. Yes, I'm with the Metropolis Police Department now."

"It's all right, Hannah," Doctor Myers called to his wife. "It's the police. They caught the man."

Hannah came to the door still holding Smoke. Bernie and David walked down to the street. Doctor Myers and Hannah followed. Smoke squirmed loose and leaped to Bernie's shoulder. Three police cars, lights flashing, surrounded a black Buick with a Hertz Sticker on the side window. Chuck Lewis leaned against it, hands cuffed behind his back.

"Father Snoop and Doctor Myers! Good to see you. Tell these goons who I am. I was just driving by on my way back to Metropolis and thought I'd stop to say hello. I saw some guy jump in his car and take off like a bat out of hell. Next thing I knew I was surrounded by police cars."

Bernie listened while his Senior Warden tried to talk himself out of this jam. Finally, Bernie said, "Why did you kill her, Chuck?"

"What are you talking about? You've let your grief push you over the edge, Snoop."

"No, Chuck. You killed Miriam. Why?"

"Don't be stupid, old man. I was in San Francisco at a conference. My wife led the board meeting that night."

"I know Patricia led the meeting, but you weren't out of town. I'm sure she thought you were, but you needed to kill Miriam before she recognized you. She missed the first Sunday because of the flu, so she didn't see you. She hadn't seen the list of members or the pictorial directory, so she didn't know you were involved in our church. But, why after all these years? Did you carry a grudge that long?"

"You don't know what you're talking about. I was in San Francisco. I have an envelope full of receipts for meals and books from the conference."

"I'm sure you do, but someone else bought them in your name, just like someone else stayed in the room you reserved. But unless you drove – and you didn't – how did you get from Metropolis to San Francisco?"

"I flew. Ask Patricia. She took me to the airport."

"We did ask her," said Hollohan. "She didn't stay to see you off. We checked all flights. You weren't on any of them, but you did rent a car – under the alias C. J. L-o-u-i-s."

"Why?" Bernie again asked. David stood beside him, a hand on his shoulder – the one not occupied by Smoke.

Suddenly, Chuck looked beaten and angry. "No one gives me the boot and gets away with it. I didn't know if she'd told you about us, but it didn't matter. I had to talk to her before my wife learned the woman I really loved was our pastor's wife. I went to the house and let myself in. I thought she would be in the kitchen. She wasn't. She called out from the parlor – thought it was you home early. She was surprised and angry to see me. She said you didn't even know the name of her fiancé because it didn't matter. That made me even more angry. It was bad enough she threw me away like an old shoe, but then to say I didn't matter at all! I slapped her and she fell. She hit her head. I reached to help her up, but she was dead. I didn't intend to hurt her. I just wanted to talk." His voice fell to barely a whisper. "You couldn't have loved her as much as I did."

"In all the years we were together, I never once struck her. That's love," said Bernie, his tightly clenched fists in his pockets. As much as he itched to throttle Chuck Lewis, he would not stoop to the level of a cold-blooded murderer. "Her death might have been an accident, but you went there intending to kill her."

"You can't prove that!"

"You planned every detail, including framing me. No, Mr. Lewis, you didn't love her; you coveted her. You wanted what she could give to you. I wanted her for what we had together – and we did have a wonderful ten years with never a backward glance. I want to hate you for taking her life, but then I would lose all that we had together. I can only pity you and hope that you can find peace with God for your sins."

Bernie turned away then turned back. "And, why did you kill Father Jones? Because he asked you to step down as Senior Warden?"

"Who told you that? No one was in the building – unless that gossip-monger of a secretary was snooping around."

"No, it wasn't Alice. It was Father Jones. I read his last reports. He said he was going to ask you to step down because you were too heavy-handed."

"So what? That don't prove anything."

"The note was written the afternoon he had his fatal fall down a set of stairs he had used for twenty years. What did you do? Trip him? Push him? And why did you set the fire at the church? To kill me, or scare me off before I put two and two together and learned the truth?"

"You think you're so smart, Snoop." The name slithered between the sneering lips. "Well, I'll get off. I've got *power* and *money*. You got nothing – not even your beautiful wife."

"You're wrong, Lewis. Miriam's memory will always be with me. When the church learns what you have done, they will become my friends. I've got my freedom and I've got Holy Smoke, who was smart enough to save my life and keep me from doing what my instincts told me to do when I learned what you had done."

"Father Bernie," Hannah said, with tears streaming down her face, "Come break bread with us. Let yesterday fade with the sunset; let tomorrow's haze beckon us; let today be full of life and joy."

Bernie wiped the corner of his eye as he recognized one of Miriam's quotes. He turned to David. "I'll see you back at the manse tonight and we'll talk. You take care of your real job, now."

David nodded and went with Hollohan to claim their prisoner from the Oak Grove police who wanted him for destruction of property and disturbing the peace.

"Murder takes precedence," said Hollohan. "You can have him when we're finished with him –

if there is anything left to have."

"Smoke, let's go have lunch with our friends. Now we can move forward to new adventures as Miriam would want us to do."

"Meow," said Smoke and raced back to the house to follow Hannah inside.

Book II

The Casserole Caper

One

"Bernie! Welcome, welcome. Come in. Come in." Bishop John Murray stood and walked around the wide, expensive walnut desk to shake hands. A broad smile spread across his chubby face – a smile too broad and a greeting too exuberant.

"John, or is it Bishop today?" Bernie acknowledged the man.

"Sit down, Bernie. Sit down. Would you care for a cup of coffee?"

"No thanks," said Bernie as he sat in one of the leather chair in front of the bishop's desk. Smoke, Bernie's gray cat who always accompanied him, sat on the arm of the chair, eyes closed as if napping – or praying.

The bishop sat in the other leather chair facing Bernie. "How are you doing these days?" he asked.

"Come on, John, we've been friends since seminary days. You didn't ask me in for coffee or inquire about my health. What's on your mind?"

Bishop Murray laughed. "Never could fool you, could I Bernie? You're right. This isn't just a social call. As I've told you before, I can't say how sorry I am about the mess at St. Mark's. I had no idea how bad it was until… well, I never would have sent you and Miriam there had I known the circumstances. I thought you could help the church through the grief and you did a superb job of doing that. I just wish…"

"John, what are you trying to say? We both know what happened at St. Mark's was unusual. Miriam would be the first to say you did the right thing by bringing us here. None of us had any way of knowing an old flame would wreak havoc with so many lives. Forget the past. What's on your mind today?"

The bishop sat with his elbows on the chair arms, the tips of his fingers forming a tent. "Bernie, you have given four years to St. Mark's, brought them through a horrendous time of murder and chaos. The people have accepted you and loved you – and yes probably feel some guilt over Miriam's death. But over all, you have been the loving caring pastor I knew you would be. I hope I'm not doing the wrong thing again, but I would like for you to move."

Bernie sat quietly, waiting. *Now what?*

When he didn't comment, John continued. "You have always served small towns until you came to Metropolis. I know that is what you like. What I have is mind is very different. The parish is five small villages and a small town. Very unusual names – Thumb Nail, Pointer's Grove, Middle Digit, Ringer, Pinkie's End and Martinsburg. The first five are villages at the tip of the inlets of Five Fingers Lake in the southern end of the state."

"What's the trouble there?" asked Bernie.

John laughed. "No trouble, Bernie. Their pastor retired and they need someone to fill the void."

"Really rural?"

"As rural as you can get."

"No cities?"

"None. Martinsburg is the largest town of about 15,000. That is where the church and parsonage are. The only time you would see a city is when you come to see me. If you want to think it over…"

"No need," said Bernie. "You're right. I've never liked city living. At least the nearest thing to murder down there would be meeting a bear or catching a trout."

"Then you'll go?"

"When?"

"We'll give you one month. Is that enough time?"

"We'll be ready," said Bernie. "Right Smoke? Want to go to the country where you can go outside when you want to?"

"Meow?" said Smoke as if asking, "What is a country?"

Bernie left the bishop's office with a lighter step than he'd had since Miriam's death. It would be hard to leave the few friends he had made here, but he looked forward to making new ones in a new location.

Two

While Bernie was saying goodbye to his friends and preparing to leave Metropolis, crickets along Beaver Creek in the Five Fingers Lake region tuned their chirpy violins for their nocturnal symphony. Owls hooted across the valley. Frogs in the surrounding swampy grounds strummed the bass. Occasionally, a whippoorwill added a mournful note or two. All was peaceful and usual belying any hint of danger or discord.

Suddenly silence fell mid-chord. Sensing danger animals fled noiselessly, birds crouched warily on tree branches and in nests. The peaceful night was about to become violent. Humans approached the covered bridge over Beaver Creek.

The cautious woman laid her bike on its side under the bridge and climbed the slippery bank to the road. Moving under the roof of the bridge, she waited nervously, emitting a scent of fear to the surrounding animal life.

Minutes later, a man approached from across the meadow near the swamp. A tiny red glow flickered as he stepped inside the covered bridge. A puff of smoke followed. The man grabbed the cigarette from the woman's hand and flipped it into Beaver Creek.

"What are you trying to do?" He growled. "You want someone to see us?"

"I was nervous with all the noises out here. I don't like it out in this godforsaken place." The woman's voice quivered with fear.

"Don't be stupid," he said. "I don't hear anything. There's nothing here to hurt you. If someone from town happens to be going by here and sees that cigarette, that's a different story. We would be in hot water up to our ears. Where's your car?"

"I rode my bike. It's under the bridge."

"What was so important we couldn't wait for our regular meeting night?"

"I wanted to tell you, there won't be any more regular nights. I can't take this sneaking around anymore. Bub is getting suspicious. I'm sure your wife is too. I don't like the way she looks at me when we meet downtown."

"What are you saying? That you're dumping me?"

"Not dumping, just...our...thing has...run its course."

"You got someone else waiting in the wings?"

"Of course not." Her voice rose – a note of

panic.

"No one dumps me," he said between clenched teeth. "We'll call it quits when I say so and not one second before." He twisted her arm and pulled her close to him, covering her mouth with his. She struggled to get away from him.

"Please, don't..."

The man drew back his fist, paused then dropped his arm. "Aw, forget it. Go creeping back to him. I can get someone else anytime I want to." He slapped her again. She slumped to the floor, covered her face with her hands and wept.

"Women. You're all the same." He turned and stomped off the bridge.

The woman sat for a few minutes then slid down the bank to get her bike. A man suddenly caught her and swung her around to face him. Before she could scream, he had his other hand on her throat squeezing until she lost consciousness. Then he threw her into the water and set a heavy booted foot on her head until she stopped struggling.

He stood still, listening. *What was that? Did I hear something?*

A beaver swam toward the dam. The man relaxed. *Stupid beaver.* He pushed her bike up the slope and rode it back to his car. He shoved it into the trunk and tied the lid down then drove away. His mind whirled, looking for a way to end this mess – forever.

Tentatively the midnight symphony resumed. Owls called out, "Hoo, Hoo?" Nature returned while Five Fingers' Lake townspeople slept as if tomorrow would be another ordinary day.

Three

While someone shattered the silence in the Five Fingers Lake region, Father Bernard Snoop packed the last of his books for the moving van. He had already packed his VW to the hilt. Tomorrow he and Holy Smoke would strike out for a new appointment. Since Miriam's death, he was alone, except for Smoke, his fifteen pound, smoke gray cat – and he would stay that way. They would leave before the van to make sure all was ready when it arrived at Martinsburg where the parsonage was for the parish.

The manses in Oak Grove and in Metropolis were fully furnished, but St. John's Parish wasn't. St. Mark's in Metropolis decided to refurnish the manse for the new pastor, so they gave Bernie whatever he wanted to take with him.

The women of the church would of course offer him all kinds of casseroles, begin lining up eligible women and start the dance of matchmaking. He would pretend he was hard of hearing, blind and didn't understand what they were doing. Bernie, as his friends called him, when they didn't call him

Snoop, sighed and picked up Smoke. "Better grab us a few hours of sleep," he said. "Long drive tomorrow."

*　　*　　*

Before the sun was completely over the horizon, Bernie placed the cat in the passenger seat and squeezed into his '69 VW. As he turned on the highway, he said, "Well, Smoke, we're on our way. What do you think? Will this be a quiet little community, or does the name belie a sinister existence behind it?"

"Meow?" Smoke began and continued to chatter to Bernie as if he understood thoroughly what the man said and vice versa.

"Of course, there is no reason to believe there is crime or intrigue here, but my snoopy sense tells me all communities have hidden secrets."

"Meow."

"Well, if there is, we'll find it." Bernie laughed and Smoke covered his mouth with a paw as if snickering. All Bernie's friends knew he couldn't pass on a chance to snoop out possibilities. After all, he had helped solve many crimes over the years, including his wife's murder four years ago.

*　　*　　*

The next afternoon, Bernie pulled off the expressway onto Highway 101. A lone gas station waited like a lighthouse on the seacoast. "I'll fill up here and check my map," he said to Smoke. Before he hardly turned the key off, a young man ran from the building.

"Hi," said the sandy-haired youth. "Can I fill her up for you? Clean your windows?"

Bernie opened his door and stood beside the young man. With his six feet three inch frame, he was looking down at the young man. "That's very generous of you," he said. "A little unusual these days."

"I know," said the young man as he uncapped the VW's gas cap, lifted the fuel nozzle and began filling the tank. "When my grandpa died, he left me this station because I helped him a lot when I was younger."

"Mighty big responsibility," said Bernie.

"Yes sir, but I'll make a go of it. It's the only gas station near Martinsburg and Finger Lakes. You just passing' through?"

"No, actually I'm heading for Martinsburg."

"My mama lives there. You visiting someone?"

"No, I'm the new priest at St. John's Episcopal Parish. Are you familiar with it?"

"Oh, yes sir." The youth grinned and extended his hand. "Fred Thompson," he said. "My Uncle Ned and Aunt June belong there. My wife and I come over when I can get the time off."

"Bernard Snoop," said Bernie, "and this is Holy Smoke," he finished as the cat leapt through the open car window to Bernie's shoulders.

"My directions send me though a place called Thumb Nail – an odd name for a town. Is it much further?"

Fred laughed. "If you look at the map," he said spreading an open map across the hood of the car, "the lake looks like a hand with five fingers extended. The founding fathers thought it would be amusing to give the villages fitting names."

Fred pointed to the lake and the extending fingers of water. "See how Beaver Creek meanders and winds around the toes of Bear Foot Mountain and on to Indian River. Between each of the fingers of the lakes is a small town: Thumb Nail, Pointer's Grove, Middle Digit, Ringer, and Pinkie's End.

"Just drive through Thumb Print and continue on until the paved highway becomes a gravel road. You will cross Beaver Creek through a covered bridge. Bear Mountain will be on your left. A larger meadow between the road and a marsh leads to the lake on the right. About a mile beyond the bridge, a road veers off to the right. Straight ahead in Pointer's Grove. Martinsburg is about a mile and a half to the right."

"Thank you, Fred, Good luck in your business. I'll see you in church someday."

"Thank you, Father, Elli and I will see you when we visit our family over there."

Back in the car, Bernie turned to Smoke. "Nice young man," he said and started the car.

"Meow," answered his companion.

*   *   *

Bernie took that as agreement and drove toward Thumb Print. Twenty minutes later, he spotted the covered bridge.

"There's the bridge, Smoke, what do you say we stop and have a look?"

Smoke responded by placing his paws on the dash and looking ahead. "Meow," he said, his ears twitching and tail thumping with excitement.

Bernie drove through the bridge, parked at the side of the road and walked back to the bridge. The late morning sun filtered through trees and danced on the water that rolled and tumbled over small stones and large boulders.

Smoke looked up at the high beams under the bridge roof. Although he was simply a gray alley cat, he often exhibited traits that suggested some Siamese in his genes somewhere. He loved high places. Bernie smiled as Smoke leaped to the side rail then to the top beam and jumped from beam to beam, tiptoeing from one side to the other. Suddenly Smoke stopped, looked down at the water rushing from under the bridge.

"What's the matter, pal? Too high up there? Don't expect me to climb up after you. Don't know if they have a fire department with a hook and ladder truck, so you'll have to…"

Smoke, heedless of Bernie's admonitions or the distance from the top of the bridge to the floor, sailed as if he were a flying squirrel landing at Bernie's feet. He trotted to the side and began digging at a crack in the floor.

"What you got there?" Bernie followed the cat and peered into the small crack. Something shiny sparkled in the sunlight. "Let me see if I can get it for you."

Taking a pen from his pocket, Bernie dug at the object and pulled out a shiny brass button. "Well, well, well," he said. "Sorry, Smoke, someone will be looking for…"

"Hey you, what are you doing in there?" Bernie had been so intent on getting the button that he had not heard the approaching car.

Four

Bernie turned to see a deputy strolling toward him. "Good morning, Deputy – or is it afternoon already? Just admiring the view. Beautiful bridge. Fine workmanship. I was just telling…"

"What you got there?" The deputy cut him off.

"I was just going to tell you…"

"I think you better come with me to the sheriff. He'll want to talk to you."

"Why would he want to talk to me? I just…"

"Shut up and get in the cruiser."

"What about my car?" Father Snoop was developing a definite dislike for this arrogant young man. Smoke agreed. His fur bushed and he hissed. The officer pulled his gun and pointed it at the cat.

"You shoot my cat, young man and I won't be responsible for what I may say or do."

"Looks like a wild one to me."

"Smoke, wait in the car," said Bernie. The cat glared at the officer, swished his tail at him then loped to the car and sailed through the open window. "Now, young man, if you want me to see your sheriff, I am willing to do that, but I will drive my car and follow you to town. If that is not acceptable, you will have to arrest me and I can promise you a very nasty law suit for false arrest."

Bernie drew himself up to his six foot three inches, squared his usually stooped shoulders and set his dark eyes on the deputy. The deputy, barely five and a half feet tall, hesitated, shifted from one foot to the other and glared back. Finally, lowering his gaze under the unblinking stare of Father Snoop, he motioned to his car. "You try to take off and I'll…"

"What? Shoot me? Kill my poor antique VW? Just don't drive too fast or I'll not be able to keep up." Bernie turned on his heel, walked slowly and deliberately to his car where he folded his tall frame into the driver's seat and started the engine. He winked at Smoke, who covered his mouth with a paw as if laughing at them.

"Well, Smoke, this is a first. Arrested for looking at a bridge. Sounds like this is going to be an intriguing appointment after all. Wonder what the folks at St. John's Parish will have to say about this kind of reception."

The deputy, following his instructions to the nth degree, drove about ten miles per hour the entire two and a half miles to Martinsburg. He parked in front of the County Jail and Court House, got out and swaggered over to Father Snoop's VW.

Bernie ignored him as he unfolded himself out of the car. "Coming, Smoke?" He leaned down for the cat to take his customary place on the broad shoulders. The Deputy motioned for him to go ahead of him. "You can't take that...animal in there," he said.

Father Snoop again ignored the man, walked around him and opened the door to a large lobby with glossy stone floors and brick walls. A row of elevators lined the back wall and a long, narrow corridor extended on either side of the elevators. A sign with an exaggerated black arrow indicated the hall on the left was county offices while the one of the right was the Incarceration Headquarters.

Without waiting for the deputy, Bernie started down that corridor until he found the door that had the word Sheriff's Office printed in bold, black letters. He already had the door open and was in the room when the deputy finally caught up with him. A middle-aged man, good physical shape, green eyes and rust colored hair with streaks of white, looked up from his cluttered desk.

Bernie thought the sheriff looked familiar, but before he could speak, the deputy spit out the angry accusation.

"Sheriff, I found this stranger nosing around the bridge. Thought it was mighty strange after the trouble we had there."

The sheriff gave his deputy an exasperated look. "Did you get a name? Ask why he was there?"

"Don't matter. He's a stranger to these parts and we all know that Mitchell woman wasn't murdered by a local."

"Murder?" The appointment suddenly got much more interesting. Father Snoop lifted his eyebrows in question.

"Meow?" Holy Smoke added his question.

"Parker, that was Monday. Today is Thursday. If this man is the murderer, then why is he still hanging around? And why hasn't anyone seen him?"

Father Snoop liked this sheriff. He seemed to have his head on straight and thought logically. His veiled rebuke didn't faze Deputy Parker.

"Anyone can see he's not too bright. Probably wanted to see the scene again and…"

"Careful Parker," said the sheriff, "you're treading on mighty thin ice over turbulent legal waters. Those are libelous words. Why don't we talk to the man first – see what he has to say?" With that, he stood and walked over to the dividing counter top with a legal pad and pen. He looked at Father Snoop with a hint of recognition. "Do I know you?"

"Don't think so, but you do look familiar to me. I just arrived in town. Matter of fact Smoke and I stopped to look at the marvelous covered bridge on our way into town."

The sheriff glanced first at Bernie and then the cat and then he smiled. "Holy Smoke. I thought I knew you."

The deputy's face crumpled into a frown. "What are you talking about? How can you know this man?"

"The cat's name is Holy Smoke. This is Father Bernard Snoop, new pastor at St. John's Episcopal Parish. Am I right?"

Father Snoop grinned and stretched a hand across the counter. "That's right, but I'm afraid you have the advantage."

"Sorry about that Father. I'm Sheriff Odis Law." He grinned at the expression on the preacher's face. "Yeah, I know. I get ribbed a lot about my name. Bet you do too."

"Maybe we both live up to them," said Bernie. "Where did we meet?"

"Oak Grove five years ago. I took a class you were teaching at the College on looking for the impossible. Wouldn't expect you to remember me."

"Ah, yes, the red head who always sat in the back row. Didn't have much to say, but when you did, it was always on target. Always wondered what happened to the students in that class and if any of them really learned anything. I only taught that one semester. Filling in for a friend."

"Believe me I got a lot out of the class. I wondered if the Father Snoop who was coming to town was the same one. Could sure use your help around here."

Father Snoop and Sheriff Law both turned as the deputy started choking. Sheriff Law laughed and Father Snoop patted the man on the back. Smoke jumped on the counter out of the way.

"Don't worry about him, Father. He's just choking on his words. Joe Parker, my right hand deputy. A little too quick to jump to conclusions sometimes, but basically a good law man."

"Sorry, Father," Parker muttered.

"No problem, son," he said. "Oh, by the way, you wanted to know what I had, but we got into a battle of wills and I never said." He pulled the button from his pocket and handed it to the sheriff. Smoke found this in a crack on the bridge floor. Sun must have hit it just right to draw his attention. You mentioned a murder at the covered bridge. Might be a clue – might not."

"We found Cherrie Mitchell's body in Beaver Creek under the bridge Tuesday morning. She'd drowned – with some help. Can't figure out how she got there, or why. Mitchell's live on the other end of town. She was the organist at the Methodist Church across from the Episcopal Parish church. Real blow to the community as well as her church."

"She married?"

"Yes, fifteen years. Her husband, Don, owns and operates Mitchell's Market. Hard workers and good folks. No children."

"This button has a drop of something dark on it – might be blood – like from a scuffle of some kind. Might be able to trace it to someone."

"I'll have the boys in the forensic lab take a look."

"You have a lab? I'm impressed."

Sheriff Law laughed. So did Parker. "We do and we don't," said the sheriff. "We've got a pretty well up-to-date clinic in town and a doctor – Susan Brown – who loves research. There's barely enough people in the Five Fingers Lakes villages to keep her busy, so she works extra for us in testing and research."

"Nice arrangement. Does she do surgery and veterinary work too?"

"Not exactly. We have a heliport to send emergency patients to larger hospitals. But her husband, Harold, is the county veterinarian. They help each other in many things."

"Hear that Smoke? You aren't going to miss your yearly physical after all."

Holy Smoke chattered to him in a tone that sounded an awful lot like things he shouldn't even know about, much less be saying. "Holy Smoke! That's enough of that kind of language."

Sheriff Law and Deputy Parker laughed. Smoke glared as only a cat can glare.

"I'll give your problem some thought,' said Bernie. "If I come up with anything, I'll give you a call. Now, I need to find that parsonage and get my stuff sorted and settled. I expect the van is already here."

"I heard it rumble through town during the night," said the sheriff. "They probably slept in the truck until morning."

Five

The movers were already unloading Bernie's household goods when he and Smoke parked behind the truck. "Looks like they are way ahead of us," said Bernie.

"Meow," answered Smoke. He leaped over Bernie and headed for the truck to nose around and to supervise the procedure.

"Hey, be careful with that table. It's an antique." Bernie called to the two men moving the table from the truck. He stood aside to let the movers take the heavy oak table to the house.

"Sure it is," muttered one of the men, "like some people I know."

Bernie stood and watched them for a few minutes then decided to have a look around the outside of the house. The church was next door. *I'll go over there later this afternoon.*

"Come on Smoke, let's…" Smoke wasn't with him. "Now where did that cat get to?" he muttered as he started looking. Then he saw him in the truck. "Holy Smoke, get out of there," he yelled.

All three of the movers stopped and looked at

the pastor. "Are you talking to us?" asked the younger one. "Don't you want this sofa in here?"

"Sorry," said Bernie as he picked Smoke up and placed him on his shoulders. "I was talking to my cat. He was climbing around in your truck. Just trying to get him out of your way."

"Your cat?"

"His name is Holy Smoke," said Bernie. "Come on Smoke, let's take a little walk and get out of their way."

Bernie grinned as he started across the yard. He had seen the smiles on the faces of the three movers. "Guess they really didn't want us there anyway. We'll rearrange things later. Uh oh. Heaven help us, here comes the welcome committee."

"Meow," Smoke added in his best grumbling voice.

"Father Bernard," called one of the three chubby women who approached. "Welcome to our community and our church."

"Good afternoon, ladies," he said tipping his hat and bowing slightly toward them. Smoke dug in his claws to keep from falling off his shoulders. "The name however is Snoop. Bernard Snoop and this is my live-in companion, Holy Smoke."

The woman's face turned a bright shade of apple red – whether from her goof about his name, or his offhand comment about a live-in companion. "I'm sorry...I thought...I mean..."

"What she means," spoke up the one who wore such an amazing hat that Bernie was sure it must have been a real bird's nest at one time. Smoke stretched his neck to get a better look.

"What she means," said the third member of the trio, "is that we thought Roscoe was teasing us. He's always doing that. Roscoe is the Assistant Warden of the Parish. He's the one the bishop called with information about you. He's a jokester...Roscoe, not the bishop...so, naturally we thought..."

"Yes, I'm sure there was some confusion," broke in Father Snoop. The woman, whom he thought looked like an albino magpie, would probably talk until sundown and beyond, if he didn't stop her.

"Snoop sounds so...so..." The woman stopped as if unsure how to proceed.

"Snoopy?" Father Snoop offered. "I don't mind if you call me Father Bernie, but Snoop is a very fine name. This is Holy Smoke." He stroked Smoke's sleek back as he spoke his name

"Meow," said Smoke and tried to bat at the bird's nest hat.

"Do you ladies have names?" asked Bernie. "Or shall I call you the three Welcome Sisters."

The three women giggled like schoolgirls,

although they were all in their advanced fifties or sixties. "I'm Lucinda Bates, Secretary of the church," said the woman who still had the apple colored cheeks, "Lucy for short. This is Gilda Perkins, head of the Altar Guild." She nodded toward the magpie. "And that is Mavis Potts. Mavis is in charge of the kitchen. She is one of the best cooks in the church."

"Now, Lucy, all our women are good cooks. Portia Preston makes the best chicken casseroles this side of Bear Foot Mountain. But, you'll find that out for yourself, Father Snoop. We're having one of our famous potluck dinners in your honor tomorrow evening. The entire community is invited. You don't need to worry about making anything since you don't have a wife to cook for you. There'll be plenty and you're welcome to take home the leftovers."

Mavis beamed as if she had just delivered a million dollar prize to him. Before Bernie could say anything, Lucy broke in. "I'm sure you have plenty to do, so we won't keep you. We brought a tray of sandwich makings for your lunch today. Someone will bring a casserole for your dinner tonight. I'm in the office Monday through Friday from nine to three. When you're ready, I'll be glad to go over any questions you might have."

"Thank you ladies, I do appreciate your

thoughtfulness. I will put this in the refrigerator." Smoke eyed the cold cuts from his shoulder perch. He tentatively tapped the plastic covering. "Never mind," said Bernie. "You'll get your share," he said. *And probably more. A party of ten could eat for a week from it.*

"Back already?" said one of the movers as Bernie started into the house.

"Just passing through to the refrigerator," Bernie said. "The ladies of the church just brought a tray of cold-cuts and buns for my lunch – enough for everyone. Help yourselves when you're hungry. I'm a vegetarian and don't eat most of the things on this tray."

"Really?" The younger of the men looked at the tray with interest.

"Really. Help yourselves."

"Let me take that to the kitchen for you," said the young mover. "You can get back to your walk."

"Thank you, young man. Just save a few slices of meat for my cat. He doesn't share my vegetarian tastes" The youth took the tray and started for the kitchen, snagging a piece of salami before placing the tray in the refrigerator.

Bernie and Smoke went around the back of the house and walked down to the small stream that scalloped the edge of the property. It was a beautiful day to walk and think things through.

"John told me they don't have covered dish

dinners here," he said to Smoke, who jumped down to explore the area around the creek. "I asked specifically. He knows I hate casseroles. Next time I'll have to be more specific. What he didn't say was they have the dinners but call them potluck instead of covered dish. Ah well, I'll survive once they get used to the idea that I don't eat chicken, beef or any other meat."

Six

The following evening, Father Snoop put on his derby and walked toward the door. "Smoke," he used his sternest, listen-to-me voice, "stay here and look after things. I'll bring you a scrap of chicken."

"Meow?" Smoke half closed his blue eyes, hung his head and looked up at Bernie, reminding him of a child begging for special privileges.

"Sorry, but you can't go to the dinner. People don't like animals around food."

Smoke slowly poured himself onto his side, stretched then rolled over like a playful puppy. Bernie laughed and touched the cat's tummy with the toe of his shoe. "Playing cutesy won't change a thing. Stay home."

Bernie closed the door and looked across the connecting parking lot, where cars and trucks were already letting women carrying baskets of food off at the church door. Heaving a deep sigh, he walked across the front porch that stretched the full width of the house, down the three steps to the sidewalk that connected with the driveway and crunched across the gravel lot. One of the women balanced a cake carrier in one hand, a picnic basket in the other and struggled to open the door to the fellowship hall.

"Here, let me get that for you," said Bernie hurrying to pull the door it toward him.

"Thank you, Father," she said. "I'm Gilda Perkins. I thought my husband, Roscoe was right behind me, but I see him over there with the other men. They like to stand around and chew the fat – never call it gossip – while we women get the dinner on the table."

"Glad to help out," he said. "Maybe I should go over and see what kind of fat they are chewing on this evening."

Gilda laughed and Father Snoop ambled over to the men gathered in the corner of the parking lot. One quickly dropped the cigarette he was smoking and crunched it into the gravel with the heel of his shoe. "Evening folks," said Bernie. "Guess you all know who I am, but I'll introduce myself anyway. Father Bernard Snoop. You can call me Father, Bernie, Snoop or any combination of the above." He stretched out his hand to shake hands with the group of men.

One by one the men introduced themselves – names that Bernie tried to remember, but knew it would take several times of hearing them before he did so. Sheriff Law joined them. He still had his uniform shirt and pants on, but had left his gun locked in the glove compartment of his car.

"Find out any more about who killed Mrs. Mitchell?" asked one of the men, whom Bernie thought was Sam Preston. "Probably some tramp passing through."

"Might be, Sam," said Odis. "We're working on it. Don't understand why she was way over at the bridge in the middle of the night or how she got there. No car. Not even a bicycle."

"Maybe someone stopped by her house and picked her up," said Alex Vroom, the church custodian.

"Maybe."

"Darn shame," said Robert Potts. "She was a nice lady."

"Yeah, Gilda and I went to the funeral home before we came here," said Roscoe. "Don's taking it pretty hard. Offered us some coffee, though. Always the gentleman."

"I never had that before," said Sam, "the coffee that is. Old man Wilson always has a pot on for wakes, but no one ever bothered to offer it to us before – specially the one in mourning. Portia and I accepted it, but felt strange drinking coffee at a wake."

"Yeah." Alex laughed. "Something stronger is usually the drink of choice." He laughed again.

"Well, that coffee didn't need anything in it.

Mighty strong and bitter – even with three sugars."

"They're going to miss her over across the street," said Jacob Barr nodding at The Methodist Church. She was their piano – he pronounced it *pie-ana* – player."

"Maybe we can lend them one of ours," said Alex, elbowing Roscoe who stood next to him.

Jacob glared. "Well, certainly not Orpha. My wife's been organist at our church since she was a teen-ager and I wouldn't begin to tell anyone how many years ago that was."

"Well, they can't have Melody." Nathan Ames glared at Jacob, who had been trying to get rid of Melody Ames as piano player ever since she started playing. Everyone knew Melody was better than Orpha.

"Looks like Mavis is motioning for us to come in," said Roscoe in time to thwart an unpleasant discussion. "We better go. Don't want the food to get cold – especially Portia's chicken casserole. You gotta have a big helping of that, Father. Best chicken casserole in the county."

"So I've heard," said Bernie without offering further comment. He would handle the food when the time came.

When it was almost time to begin, Roscoe raised his hands for quiet. "Folks we are sure glad to see all of you here tonight – especially our visitors and friends from the community. Looks like we have a full house tonight. As soon as everyone finds a seat and is quiet, I'll introduce our new pastor. Since the occasion is in honor of Father Bernard Snoop, I'll ask him to bless the food. Then we'll go down both sides of the tables. Help yourselves. Seconds as long as they last and…"

A very loud wail like a baby in distress sent a shiver across shoulders and down spines.

"What was that?" said Roscoe. Hair stood on end and everyone looked to Bernie to explain, since he was the pastor and should have the answers to such strange happenings. If he didn't, surely Odis Law would.

"Holy Smoke," groaned Bernie. The sound came again accompanied something gray thumping against the glass door.

"Had a Siamese cat in heat once that sounded like that," said someone across the room. "Maybe…"

"Not in heat," said Bernie, "but close. That's my cat Holy Smoke. He thinks he should go everywhere I go. I closed the door – which doesn't mean much to him. He wants to meet you."

"Aw, let him in," someone said. Others joined the chorus, singing to the tune of Bringing in the Sheaves – "Let him in, let him in, let him in to taste the casseroles…" They had to improvise a little to make the words fit. Everyone laughed and one of the children ran to the door and opened it. Holy Smoke sashayed in and leapt to Bernie's shoulders where he said, "Meow," and bowed his head for the prayer. They laughed again and Father Snoop quieted them with the prayer of blessing.

"Smoke, you'll have to get off my back until I can get us some food. We don't want to drop kitty hairs in the casseroles, now do we?"

Smoke jumped to the floor, covered his mouth with his paw and made a noise that sounded like he was snickering. Father Snoop went first in line and took a small piece of chicken for Smoke, then filled his plate with something from all the vegetable dishes on the table. He started back to sit and Sam Preston stopped him.

"You didn't get any of Portia's chicken casserole, Father," he said. "She'll be awfully disappointed if you don't eat her casserole."

"Thank you," said Bernie, "but my plate is full." He turned to go. Sam grabbed his arm and pulled him back.

"You got room right there," he said, pointing to a small bare spot on the plate.

"The truth is," said Bernie looking into the angry, flashing eyes of Sam Preston, "I'm a vegetarian. I don't eat chicken casseroles." He was afraid Sam would have a stroke on the spot.

"What do you mean you don't eat chicken

casseroles?" His voice rose with each word "Why I never heard of a preacher who don't eat chicken. It's downright unchristian to turn down Portia's..."

"Let it go, Sam." Odis Law laid a hand on his arm. "Ain't worth raising a fuss over. You don't want to ruin your wife's dish for others."

Sam glared, took a double helping of the casserole and went to sit as far from the preacher as possible. Bernie sighed. *They'll get used to it.* He cut up the piece of chicken for Smoke, placed it on a small desert plate and set it on the floor beside him. The rest of the meal went very well, except for the side-glances and head shaking across the room.

Soon it was time for the evening program, but when Roscoe rose to ask folks to go to the sanctuary, he looked pale. "I'm sorry," he said. "Someone else will have to handle the program. I'm not feeling so well." He threw his hand over his mouth and raced to the men's room. Unfortunately, so did several others. They turned and ran out the door. Women didn't run, but they moved as quickly as they could. Within minutes two thirds of the folks were either in the rest rooms, parking lot or side lawn heaving.

Bernie looked at Odis Law. "Better call for medical assistance. Looks like food poisoning of some kind. I'll get folks who aren't heaving into the sanctuary out of the way and begin listing what everyone ate. You can tend to the rest."

"Thanks Father. Luckily you and I are all right..." A loud scream interrupted him. Portia Preston stood screaming one long, loud banshee scream after another. Sam was lying face down in his plate, not moving.

By ten o'clock, Sheriff Law had sent home any who were well enough and had given their statement. The able-bodied men had pushed aside the tables and threw mats on the floor for makeshift beds until the sick felt settled enough to leave. The paramedic vehicle took Sam Preston's body to the clinic where Dr. Brown would do an autopsy later that night – or early the next morning.

Midnight found Bernie, Law, Parker and Lucy Bates drinking coffee in Bernie's office comparing notes. Lucy had volunteered to stay and help correlate the dishes. First, they listed all the dishes sampled by persons not taken ill. One by one, they eliminated each dish from the list of those who were ill, until finally only three dishes remained on the list of foods eaten by all those who became ill – Portia's chicken casserole, Gilda's beef and mushroom casserole, and Mavis' ham and potato casserole.

"We left all the dishes on the table downstairs," said Parker. "Want me and Lucy to gather samples from each of those dishes? She knows which ones we need."

"Why don't we all go down, then we'll call it a day." Sheriff Law stood and stretched.

While Parker and Law gathered the samples from the dishes Lucy showed them, Bernie did what he enjoyed most. He snooped. Smoke at his side, he checked out every dish and place still on the tables. He glanced around the rest of the room and noticed a jacket hanging on the coat rack.

"It's Sam's," said Lucy, when she saw him walk toward it.

"I thought I saw him wearing it earlier," Bernie said. Smoke sat on a chair batting at the sleeves. *Holy Smoke doesn't play with anything like that without a reason.*

"What we got here, Smoke?"

The cat chattered to him as if answering the question. He batted the sleeve once more for emphasis. Bernie lifted the hanging appendage and fingered the button-less thread between two brass buttons.

"Sheriff," he called, "I think we got a match."

"A match?" Sheriff Law trotted over to the coat rack and took a look at the sleeve Bernie held up for him. "Sure looks like the one you found at the bridge. Looks like we found us a murderer, but who murdered the murderer? Or was it simply coincidence and poetic justice?"

"Depends on whether this was food poisoning or something else?"

"Someone would have to be desperate to take a chance on killing a whole room full of people just to make a murder look like an accident."

"Murderers are desperate," said Bernie. "How'd you do with the samples?"

"There was plenty of everything except Portia's chicken casserole. The dish was empty. We're taking the dish. Figured Doc could find a trace of something if anything is there."

"Good thinking. In the meantime, I'll visit with the three women first thing in the morning. Need to console the widow, anyway. See what I can learn."

Seven

Knowing farmers were early risers, Bernie was on the doorstep of the Preston home before many folks were even thinking about getting up.

"Father Snoop," said a teary-eyed Portia. "It was so good of you to call. I don't know what I'll do without Sam. He did everything for me."

"It is such a loss – and to happen the way it did. Something must have been tainted."

"Probably Gilda's beef and mushroom dish. I keep telling her to be careful with the kind of mushrooms she uses. She likes to go out in the woods and gather wild ones – gives dishes a better flavor she says. Probably got a bad one in the bunch. Poor Sam, he loved wild mushrooms too."

"He really loved your chicken casserole," said Father Snoop. "Got a little irate with me because I'm a vegetarian."

"You are? I didn't know that. Yes, Sam was very fanatical about...everything. Wanted things just the way he wanted them and no other."

"Did he hunt mushrooms often?"

"Oh, no, he never looked for them. Said he

wouldn't know a good one from a bad one."

"Did he like to fish?"

"No. Said it was a waste of time?"

"Did he just like to walk in the woods and across the creek?"

"He hated walking anywhere without a reason. Never went to the bridge."

"Never? That's odd."

"What's odd?

"I found a button to his jacket sleeve on the covered bridge when I was coming into town yesterday. Actually my cat, Holy Smoke, found it because it was a shiny brass one." Bernie watched as the color drained from her face. Suddenly her head dropped into her open hands. She began to weep.

"Want to talk about it? He was cheating on you, wasn't he?"

She nodded. "I followed him that night when he went to meet her. I heard them inside the bridge. She said she didn't want to see him anymore. He laughed at her – the way he laughed at me when I said I wanted out of our lousy marriage. I couldn't stand to see or hear any more so I ran back home. It was another hour before he came home. The next morning, when we heard about Cherrie Mitchell, he acted surprised. I wondered how could do such a thing to a nice girl like that and decided I would help God take care of it one way or another."

"What did you put in the casserole?"

"Just a little syrup of ipecac. I knew it wouldn't hurt anyone – just make them sick."

"How did it kill him?"

"I don't know. I didn't intend to kill him – just scare him."

Portia looked at me with eyes full of tears, wide and pleading. "What will they do with me?"

"I don't know, Portia, but we live in a fair community. It was an accident, but we need to talk to Sheriff Law. Do you want me to go with you?"

"Would you do that? Even knowing what I've done? And you not even here two days?"

"You are one of my flock, Portia. I'll not desert you. God said, 'Vengeance is mine,' and 'forgive your brother as I have forgiven you.' Come, we'll work it out."

*   *   *

Later that morning Bernie sat with Portia in the sheriff's office. "I didn't really mean to kill him," she said and dabbed at the tears rolling down her cheeks. "I just wanted to scare him so he would stop running around on me and stop punching me.

"Sam beat you?"

"Sometimes…I knew it was wrong but I was too scared to say anything to anyone. Who would believe me?"

"So you took a chance of killing a whole

congregation to make him listen to you?" Sheriff Law wasn't nasty, but neither was he compassionate.

"I didn't think it would kill anyone. I ate some too. I was as sick as the rest."

Bernie had been listening trying to make sense of it. Something wasn't fitting. "She has a point, Sheriff," he said. "If it was powerful enough to kill a man the size of Sam Preston, how come it didn't kill some of the children who only got sick?"

"Maybe he ate more than the rest."

"I saw Roscoe go back for seconds, maybe thirds."

"Maybe..." the phone interrupted. "Yeah, Sheriff Law speaking. Yeah, Doc. What you got for me?...Uh huh...Un huh...You don't say? Thanks."

"There was something more in him than syrup of ipecac," said Bernie.

"Yeah, barbiturates – a large quantity."

"Barbiturates? But how...what...Oh my goodness." Portia's already pale countenance became even chalkier.

"What did you put in his helping, Portia?"

"Maybe we better get you a good lawyer before you answer any more questions," said Father Snoop laying his hand on her arm.

"But I didn't have anything like that in the house – or anywhere else. Neither one of us ever took strong medicine of any kind – nothing stronger than aspirin."

"The casserole wouldn't have gotten to his blood stream yet," said Bernie. "It would have taken a couple of hours at the least. What did he eat or drink before coming to the church?"

Portia gasped and if possible turned even whiter. "The coffee?"

"What coffee, Portia? Did you put something in his coffee?"

"No – that is yes, but…"

"Wilson's?"

She nodded and the sheriff looked first at Bernie then at Portia. "Someone want to tell me what you're talking about? Bernie told him of the conversation he'd heard before dinner. "Sam said the coffee was strong and bitter even with three sugars."

"Did you get his coffee?" Sheriff Law asked Portia.

"I started to, but Don came to help. There were three cups and he took Sam's. I started back and turned to see if he was following. He threw something in the wastebasket. I thought I left the sugar papers on the table. Sam was always cleaning up after me."

"You think Don might have put something in Sam's cup?"

"Why would he want to hurt Sam?

"Why did you?"

Portia glanced at Bernie who nodded. "Tell him everything Portia."

She told him about following Sam to the bridge. "I thought I heard someone following me and I was scared that Sam had heard or seen me. But then I didn't hear it anymore and ran as fast as I could."

"Is it possible Don followed his wife to the bridge?"

"Then why didn't he stop the man from killing his wife?" Odis rubbed his hands across his tired eyes.

"Maybe Sam didn't kill her."

"But you found his button…"

"I didn't say Sam wasn't there. We know he was. Portia saw him. The button was there. They might even have scuffled a little and he probably slapped her. But suppose he left before he let his anger push him to murder."

"But if he didn't, then…"

"The angry, jealous husband? Then he planned his revenge."

"But why? If Sam were convicted of the murder, he would have his revenge."

"But if Sam wasn't convicted – or even caught…Call Dr. Brown. Ask her if there was anything unusual about the body of Mrs. Mitchell."

While Sheriff Law and Father Snoop

deliberated, Portia sat with her mouth open following their conversation like a Ping-Pong match.

Odis replaced the phone and looked at Father Snoop with awe. "How did you know?"

"I didn't, but there must have been more to it than his wife having an affair with an older man."

"What...?" Portia's face reflected her fear.

"Mrs. Mitchell was pregnant," said the sheriff.

"Oh no," she said, "but that doesn't mean Sam..."

"Afraid it does," said Sheriff Law. "Don had an accident when he was young that left him incapable of fathering children. He never told Cherrie. She thought it was her fault they couldn't have children. When she told him she was pregnant, she was thrilled. He knew it wasn't his. That's when he must have followed her. That's when she told Sam she was through. She never knew she wasn't carrying Don's baby."

"Then he killed her because of his jealously and he killed Sam because Sam was able to give Cherrie what he couldn't," Bernie said.

"Looks that way," said Odis. He picked up the phone again and made two calls. One for a search warrant and the other to Deputy Parker to search Don's home for the drug then pick up Don Mitchell as soon as the funeral was over.

"But my casserole..."

"Don didn't know about that, but he assumed with so many dishes it would be possible for it to look like food poisoning and no one would ever suspect. He couldn't have known you would provide the motive for a thorough investigation. If you hadn't had your revenge, we wouldn't have ours," Father Snoop said.

"Since you put it that way," said Odis, "we can't fault you for helping the law. Apparently, the sickness was a combination of too much food, too much excitement and too much heat. It was a rather warm evening and inside with all that hot food and warm bodies…"

"Sheriff, what are you saying?" Portia looked confused and hopeful.

"I'm saying go home, Portia. You have some rough days ahead of you preparing for a funeral."

Father Snoop took her home. Later he would go with her to Wilson's Funeral Home to help her plan the funeral for her husband. And somehow, with that sixth sense of Snoopy preachers he knew that future pot luck dinners at St. John's would be missing three formerly favorite casseroles – Portia's chicken casserole, Mavis' ham and potatoes casserole, and Gilda's beef and mushroom casserole.

Now if he could just teach them to make some vegetarian casseroles…

ABOUT THE AUTHOR

Mary Lu (Pennock) Warstler was born in Oak Hill, West Virginia. She is a 1956 graduate of Collins High School.

In September 1957, Mary Lu married Rodney J. Warstler and became a full time Minister's wife. They have four children, nine grandchildren, and five great-grandchildren.

In 1980, Mary Lu received her B. S. in Education with a minor in music. After teaching learning disabled children for two years, she enrolled at Methodist Theological School in Ohio and received a Master of Divinity in Theology in 1985.

Mary Lu and her husband Rodney are both ordained United Methodist Ministers. On July 1, 2000, she joined her husband in retirement where she pursues other areas of ministry – primarily writing and painting. They live in Copeland Oaks Retirement Community at Sebring, Ohio.

While Mary Lu loves animals, especially cats, she has no pets since the death of her two Siamese

(Nicholas and Sugar Plum) and her "British Blue Wannbe" (Michael).

Mary Lu has written numerous worship resources, plays, sermons and novels. In her *spare* time, she enjoys reading, writing, painting, music and needlework of all kinds.

www.ingramcontent.com/pod-product-compliance
Lightning Source LLC
Chambersburg PA
CBHW070106260626
47160CB00004B/1348